Christine Merrill lives on a farm in Wisconsin, USA, with her husband, two sons and too many pets—all of whom would like her to get off the computer so they can check their e-mail. She has worked by turns in theatre costuming and as a librarian. Writing historical romance combines her love of good stories and fancy dress with her ability to stare out of the window and make stuff up.

AWAKENING HIS SHY DUCHESS

Christine Merrill

MILLS & BOON

First published in Great Britain 2023
by Mills & Boon, an imprint of HarperCollins*Publishers* Ltd,
1 London Bridge Street, London, SE1 9GF

www.harpercollins.co.uk

HarperCollins*Publishers*, Macken House, 39/40 Mayor Street Upper,
Dublin 1, D01 C9W8, Ireland

Awakening His Shy Duchess © 2023 Christine Merrill

ISBN: 978-0-263-30521-0

06/23

MIX
Paper | Supporting
responsible forestry
FSC™ C007454

This book is produced from independently certified FSC™ paper
to ensure responsible forest management.
For more information visit: www.harpercollins.co.uk/green.

Printed and Bound in the UK using 100% Renewable Electricity
at CPI Group (UK) Ltd, Croydon, CR0 4YY

To the Harmons. Thinking of you.

Chapter One

'It is probably for the best that the old Duke died. He was not a healthy man and suffered greatly. But for us it changes nothing.'

Her father was wrong. It changed everything. But Madeline Goddard offered him a vacant smile and nodded obediently. If she had learned anything in twenty years of being Mathew Goddard's daughter, it was that nothing good came of rebellion.

He continued, 'The way the marriage agreement is worded, you will be wedded to the Duke of Glenmoor before your twenty-first birthday and he will receive in dowry the land and stream that divides our properties. But the paper does not specify the name of the man, only his title.'

She nodded again, offering a moment of silent thanks that the person attached to the agreement was no longer a man still desperate for an heir at three and seventy. God rest the last Duke of Glenmoor, but if he'd wished to go through with the agreement he would have been smarter to marry her a year ago, when he'd had the strength and breath to do so. With an age difference as great as theirs, it had been unwise to wait until the last minute before she was of age and might legally refuse him. For a moment she let down her guard and shuddered at the thought of the narrow escape.

Without a word, her mother handed a shawl across the carriage to her, so she might disguise the reaction as a momentary chill.

'The new Duke will be just as good as the old, I am sure,' her father went on, oblivious to her disgust. 'Inexperienced, of course. He was not expecting to inherit and is no closer than a second cousin to the old Duke. But the bloodlines are good. And, of course, the money and land have not changed.'

The new Duke was supposed to be twenty-nine. That, at least, did not fill her with horror. And if this talk of bloodlines made her think of mares and stallions? Then she was smart enough to keep those thoughts to herself.

'The party tonight is being given in Glenmoor's honour by the Duke of Fallon. It is an interesting connection between the two men. The widowed mother of Glenmoor married the father of the current Fallon and the two men were raised as brothers. Think of that. Two dukes in the same house.'

She imagined the families for a moment as a complicated diagram of intersecting lines, the two intended straight branches of family trees veering off in unexpected directions to land two powerful men in the same family. What were the probabilities of that? Probably better than they appeared. The best families in England seemed to know each other and intermarry to a degree that was almost incestuous.

Since her father was untitled, the probability of her meeting Glenmoor was much lower than that of Glenmoor knowing Fallon. But it was increased by the few acres of Goddard land that bordered the Glenmoor holdings. The odds of meeting both dukes, as she was likely to do tonight…

While she was distracting herself with probabilities there had been a dramatic pause in the narrative that seemed to need filling. Madeline's mother supplied, 'How interesting,' and gave Maddie a gentle nudge with the toe of her slipper to remind her to contribute something.

She smiled at her father again and said, 'Indeed.'

This seemed to content him, and he continued to regale them with the details of the connection, a comparison of the holdings of the two men and the fact that they would both be like family to her.

That was the point, after all. Her marriage was supposed to make unbreakable family connections that would raise the status of all Goddards. She would be a duchess and her parents would be welcome in the finest houses in England.

As her father droned on, Madeline steadied her breath to hide any signs of the panic that seemed to grow with each mile they travelled towards London. The whole plan was madness. She should not have been expected to marry an old man she had barely known, or to change fiancés as easily as changing shoes when the first one died. Surely the new Duke would not agree to an arrangement that his predecessor had made.

Her gaze fell on the handle of the carriage door, just beside her. One jerk downward and a little push, and she would be out of the door and away from here. But since she had no destination in mind, the odds for escape were not favourable. She was more likely to stumble and become tangled in the wheels. She would injure herself, or worse.

Her father would not let a little thing like her brush with death interfere with his plans. It was easier to imagine him dragging her into the Fallon ballroom, broken and muddy, than to picture a new life somewhere far away from here, where she could plan her own future.

Of course, daydreams had never been her forte. She had a better mind for numbers than fantasy. It was more relaxing to stare into space and try to calculate pi to the last decimal than to think about a future married to a man who might be even more controlling than her father. Or perhaps not. Perhaps there would be more freedom than she had in her current life.

Freedom.

She sighed at the word, which was as much a stranger to her as the Duke of Glenmoor.

Her father paused his one-sided conversation to give her a sharp look. 'What is the matter with you, girl?'

'Nothing at all,' she said quickly. Nothing that mattered to her father, at least.

'Good,' he replied with a nod. 'You must be at your best tonight. You are about to meet the man that will change all our lives.'

Evan Bellwether had known he would be Duke of Fallon from the first moment he had known anything at all. And with that knowledge had come certain assumptions. His father had always assured him that, once he had ascended to the Dukedom, his word would be law, and no one would dare to argue with it. It was annoying to find his stepbrother, Alex, who had a title of his own, had assumed the same thing.

'I am a grown man and I do not want to get married. You can't make me.' They were in the library of Fallon Hall, just down the corridor from the ballroom. And, as usual, Alex had his nose stuck in a book, defiantly ignoring the fact that he was the guest of honour at tonight's festivities and minutes away from meeting the woman that should be his bride.

'Don't blame me,' Evan said to the back of his head. 'It was your predecessor that made the agreement.'

Alex snapped the book shut in irritation and turned to look at him. 'And cousin Theodore is not here, because he is dead. Since you are the one taking his side, you might as well have his share of the blame.'

'If the paper says the Duke of Glenmoor agreed to it, then you are honour bound, as Glenmoor, to follow through.' And as he had learned at his father's knee, bonds of honour were stronger than steel.

But though Alex was an honourable man, he had been raised to be untitled and self-interested. 'I could also make a settlement on the family of the girl for backing out,' he suggested, looking longingly at his book before setting it aside.

'You could,' Evan agreed in a doubtful tone. 'It is not exactly going back on your word. But you're the last Duke…'

'I will be doing that, then.' Alex's face split in a relieved smile as he interrupted. 'How much do you think it will take to buy my way out of this mess? I do not have a blank cheque with me, but surely an IOU will be enough to send the Goddards back to wherever it is that they came from.'

'Norfolk.' Evan sighed. It was clear that though his stepbrother understood his power in principle, he had yet to learn the smartest way to use it. 'Have you considered your cousin's reason for making the arrangement?'

'I assume the old goat wanted an heir to keep the title from falling to me,' he said with an answering sigh. 'We both knew it was a fate worse than death. And yet here we are, him dead and me…?' He frowned at the ducal signet ring on his hand as if it was somehow at fault for the current situation.

'That was one reason, but there is another. Those

Goddards you want to send packing will be returning to a small property that adjoins the Glenmoor estate. If you marry the daughter, she comes with a dowry. You stand to gain several acres of land that adjoins your property, and a small fortune that is kept in trust for the girl until the time of her marriage. The terms of the transaction are in your favour.'

'Transaction?' the other man said with a bark of laughter. 'That is what you call yoking myself to a total stranger for a lifetime?'

'That is what I call it, because that is what it is,' Evan replied, trying to manage a smile in return. 'Perhaps, as a poor schoolteacher, you thought you might be marrying for love. But you are a duke now.'

'I was not a poor schoolteacher. I was a don at Oxford.'

'And now you are one of the most powerful men in England,' Evan said, hoping that the truth would finally sink in. 'As such, your life is no longer your own. Since it is in the best interest of your estate to marry this...' he glanced down at the paper that lay on the desk between them '... Madeline Goddard, you should do so.'

'In your opinion,' Alex added, giving him the

sort of dry disapproving look that Evan had dreaded from his professors at university.

Then he remembered his age and his title, straightened his spine and proclaimed the truth. 'As someone who was raised to take on the responsibilities of a peerage, I can tell you there is no place for romance in marriage. You must only think of your need for an heir and what advantages a link to the girl's family might gain you. When the lights are out, one woman is very much like another. This one, at least, comes with land that you need.'

'Don't I have enough land?' Alex said with a tired sigh.

'More is better. And I have ridden the stretch in question, just as you should have. It has a very nice stream on it that your southern tenants are using to water their livestock. Until now you have had to pay an annual fee to Goddard for access. But that will change with the marriage.'

'Then I will buy the land without taking the girl,' Alex said, giving him the look again. 'If he is willing to give it to me now, then the right combination of time and price is likely to achieve the same ends without need for a marriage.'

Evan gave a growl of frustration. 'That is one

solution. But it does not take into account the written agreement and the girl's feelings on the matter.'

Alex laughed. 'I suspect her feelings are much like mine. Unless she is a simpleton, the thought of marrying a total stranger terrifies her.'

'A strange duke, you mean,' Evan reminded him.

Alex laughed again. 'I rather like the idea of being a strange duke. But I was thinking more of my elderly cousin, who was her first intended. The idea that he would take a young wife at his age is even more revolting than the idea that she can be bartered away again to the next man in line. If Goddard would treat his daughter in such a mercenary fashion, I want no relation to him, no matter how fine his land is.'

Evan sighed. 'If you are convinced, then there is little more I can say on the matter. But the girl and her family will be here at the ball tonight and they are expecting to meet you.'

'When they do, I will speak to the girl to assure her that I have no intention of forcing a marriage upon her,' Alex said with a finality that sounded unpersuadable. 'Now, go and greet your guests. I will join them shortly and do as I have promised with as little scandal as possible. Then we can go back to our lives and forget this ever happened.'

Chapter Two

A short time later, the Goddard carriage stopped in front of a magnificent house on the edge of the city, the white stone façade gleaming in the light of dozens of torches held by footmen in green livery trimmed with shining gold braid.

Despite her fear, Maddie felt a wave of genuine excitement at the prospect of the fabulous mansion and the food and dancing that waited inside. Though she had toured the common rooms of a few great houses, she had never been invited to a party in one, much less been an honoured guest.

Of course, this called to mind another problem. Though this house belonged to the Duke of Fallon, Glenmoor had something similar. If she married him, she would be mistress of a townhouse and a country manor. The *ton* would expect her to throw fantastic parties, just like this.

The thought was daunting. Since her family had not bothered with a coming out for her, she knew very little about the sort of gathering they were now attending, much less how to be hostess for one.

And what was she to do with a house full of servants? Their family was not poor, but neither did they live as grand as this. Her mother did not need more than a cook and a couple of maids to manage the whole of the Goddard home. A mansion of this size might have a staff ten times larger than what she was used to, all looking to her for direction.

She must hope that her duke was a very patient man, for she would have much to learn if she was to be the wife he needed.

Her duke.

They were standing at the head of the ballroom steps now, and as a footman announced the Goddard family, Maddie stared down into the crowd, trying to make out the person most likely to be the Duke of Glenmoor. At the sound of her name, one man looked up as if he had been eagerly awaiting her arrival.

She stifled a sigh as their eyes met. She was saved. If this was the man she was meant to marry, then for once fortune had smiled on her. Not just smiled but beamed with such beneficence as to make up for a lifetime of slights and disappointments.

She had told herself often enough that it did not matter what the new Duke looked like, so long as he was not old enough to be her father. But now that she had seen him, she decided it mattered very much. She wanted a husband as handsome as this man, with a firm chin and a straight nose and smooth skin with just a touch of sun-kissed bronze. With brilliant blue eyes that lit when he smiled, and a tracery of lines at the corners that hinted his smiles were frequent. With golden-blond hair that had just a bit of a wave, the sort that made her want to see him when he was due to have it cut, so that she could catch him brushing it from his forehead with an exasperated sigh.

Even in his imperfection, he would be perfect.

She smiled back at him and walked slowly down the stairs, resisting the urge to race the length of them and throw herself into his arms. As she did so, she did her best not to notice the other young ladies in the room. Many of them were more beautiful than she was and all of them were more fashionable. He must have noticed that she did not compare with the London beauties he was used to.

But it didn't really matter. She must remember

that it was all arranged. The first meeting between them was nothing more than a formality, a first step on the way to the altar.

When she reached the bottom of the stairs, she stood before him for a moment, stealing one last look before lowering her eyes and dropping into her deepest and most subservient curtsy. 'Your Grace.' Her voice had a husky quality that sounded strange in her own ears. But at least it masked the excited trembling that she feared would overtake her at any moment.

'Miss Goddard,' he responded, his tone warm and friendly. 'And Mr and Mrs Goddard as well. Welcome.' He gestured them further into the room. 'Champagne?' He waved to the nearest footman, who carried a tray of glasses.

She rose from her curtsy and gave a polite shake of her head. At home, her father did not allow her to drink un-watered wine, and she doubted he would approve of her taking anything stronger than lemonade while at such an important event as this.

'I insist,' the Duke said with a smile, then muttered something under his breath that sounded suspiciously like, 'You will need it.'

She took the glass and sipped dutifully.

He gave a nod of approval. And then the paragon

before her turned and called, 'Glenmoor!' looking expectantly across the room.

She had a moment of complete confusion as another man stepped forward, a man that was as dark as this one was fair. He was handsome enough, she supposed, with intelligent brown eyes, a nice smile and a smooth, unworried brow. He would make some woman a fine husband. But he was not what she imagined when she heard the title 'Duke', nor did he command the room the way the paragon in front of her did.

Unwillingly, her eyes strayed back to the other man, and she realised her mistake. He had greeted her as a host would, not expecting an introduction while knowing exactly who she was. And then he had summoned a servant as if he owned the house. This beautiful, magnanimous gentleman was the Duke of Fallon.

And she had been behaving like a love-struck idiot towards the wrong duke.

She downed the last of her champagne in a single gulp and forced a smile for the one who was standing before her now, the man who she was meant to marry. She was vaguely aware that Fallon, the man she did not dare look at again, was performing the introductions, and she curtsied mechanically to her fiancé, afraid to look him in the eye lest he notice her disappointment.

'Miss Goddard,' he said in a tone that sounded as awkward as she felt. 'May I have this dance?'

'Of course.' She rose and took the hand he offered, allowing him to lead her out onto the floor as the musicians struck up a waltz.

She had never waltzed before. The dance was far too intimate to be allowed in her sheltered life thus far. It was probably only appropriate because the man to partner her was the one she was supposed to marry. But though they both kept to the beat, there was something wrong in their pairing. They were like a mismatched team of horses who could not pull straight and fought in their harnesses.

Still, the Duke persevered, leading her gamely around the room until they were on the far side from her parents before pulling her off the dance floor so they might speak. He looked down at her with a relieved smile. 'Miss Goddard, my apologies. But I wanted to talk without the others interfering. This whole scheme…the two of us together…married because of a piece of paper that neither of us has signed…it is ridiculous. Do you see it?'

'Yes,' she said with an equally relieved sigh. Then she covered her mouth, for the word had escaped totally against her better judgement. It was good that her father had not been able to hear it, for she could imagine the punishment she would receive for upsetting the carefully laid plans that were meant to elevate the whole family in the eyes of society.

The Duke patted her shoulder as if he sensed her fears. 'Do not worry about what your parents will say. I will take care of everything. There will be a settlement. I will see that there is no damage to your reputation. I will find a way to put this right. Then you will be free to choose the husband you want.'

He had been doing so well up to that point. But this final statement was so far outside the bounds of probability that it made her want to laugh. Whatever happened to her now, it would not be at her choice. Just as he had before, her father would make the decision, and she would abide by it. There would be no discussion, no courtship and certainly not the mythical true love that this kind man imagined she had been waiting for.

'Thank you,' she said. He meant well, after all. She lacked the words to explain her situation to him: that this brief, failed meeting would be blamed for what came after. Nor was it in his power to save her from the beating she was likely to get when her father realised that things had gone all wrong and she would not be bringing a title back to the family to honour them all. There would be no invitations to fine dinners and balls for her mother, and no entrées to clubs for her father.

She'd had one job tonight, and she had failed in it.

Glenmoor was oblivious to the turmoil in her heart, convinced that she was as happy as he was by her escape. 'Why don't you enjoy the party while I find your father and explain things to him?' the Duke said with another charitable smile. 'There is dancing, of course, and refreshment. But if you prefer a moment to yourself, the gardens are through the door behind you. They are lovely in the moonlight.'

'That would be nice,' she said, staring at the open French doors as she had stared at the carriage doors earlier. No one knew her here. No one would notice if she ran. Her parents would not miss her for several minutes. How far away could she get before her absence was discovered?

Probably not far. But if she did not try, she would still be here, easily found and dragged home to face her mother's disappointment and her father's rage.

With a brief glance to assure herself that her parents were not watching her, she slipped through the doors and out into the night. The Duke was right;

the gardens were beautiful even in near darkness.
The air was heavy with the scent from banks of
roses stretching in paths down to an ivy-covered
wall at the bottom of a gentle slope.

Her eyes followed the expanse of stone, stretching a hundred feet in either direction. She could run
towards the stables on the left, and the carriages,
or the front of the house on the right. Either would
lead her to people who would send her back to her
parents, thinking she had lost her way.

There was a third option: straight over the wall
and into the unknown. There might be a road there.
She could walk back into the city. Once there, she
could find a friend to hide her. She thought of her
former governess, Miss Harrison, living in Cheap-
side. She had always promised that, should Maddie
be in the neighbourhood, a visit would be welcome.

Of course, she was not in the neighbourhood.
She was miles and miles away, with nothing more
substantial in her reticule than a silk handkerchief
to fund a journey through London.

All the more reason to begin walking.

She would go to Miss Harrison and beg to be hidden. Perhaps, between the two of them, they could
forge some letters of reference and she could find
her own position as a governess. She could spend

the rest of her life in a schoolroom somewhere, teaching maths to children. It was a happier ending than the idea of being married off to the next man her father decided would suit her, and definitely better than the punishment she would get if they caught her tonight.

But first she must master the fence. After one last moment of hesitation, she reached for the ivy and began to climb.

From his place near the doorway, Evan chatted absently with the Goddards, but his thoughts strayed to the girl who had gone out to the garden. Their meeting had been brief but strange. She had looked at him with such eager intensity that it had left him feeling as if a lengthy conversation had taken place, though few words had been exchanged. Her silence towards him had been full of expectation, as if she was listening to words that he had not spoken and answering them in kind.

It was probably nothing more than a flight of fancy brought on by a pair of big green eyes and the broad, guileless smile that matched them. When he had first heard about Alex's intended bride, Evan had assumed that the girl must be a bit of a quiz. If her father had made her match contingent on the exchange of land, he clearly had no faith in her ability to navigate the marriage mart and find a worthy husband using a fine face and a pleasing manner.

But Madeline Goddard had a sweet, wholesome beauty that could have won the heart of the most jaded lord. Her looks were all the more striking because they were unmarked by the artifice and desperation that one sometimes found in London debutantes as they approached twenty-one without a husband. Perhaps it was because she had thought her future was secure. If so, she had been disabused of the fact after talking with Alex.

He wondered if his brother would rethink his plans, now that he had seen the girl. It would be no hardship to marry such an appealing creature.

But it appeared not. Evan had watched their brief conversation with interest and Alex had seemed to be doing most of the talking. Miss Goddard had stood stock still and silent, taking in his rejection of her without so much as a blink. Shouldn't there have been a shower of tears? Or perhaps a whoop of relief if she was as set against the marriage as his brother had assumed?

Instead, she had been passive. It made Evan wonder if she had fully understood what had just happened to her. Or perhaps she was in shock. When

Alex had finished with her, she had drifted through the French doors and out into the garden, probably to have a well-deserved and private breakdown.

Evan could imagine in detail the girl's disappointment, though she hid it gracefully. Miss Goddard had spent years being told that her future was secure, only to have her dreams ripped apart in an instant. Since her jilting had happened in his home, he felt responsible for it, as though he had caused the hurt himself. He should do something to repair the damage, even if it was only to offer her a handkerchief to dry her tears.

Now, Alex was on his way back across the room to speak to her parents. Given the choice of further communion with Goddard or seeing to his daughter's welfare, Evan chose the girl. The man was proving to be a pompous boor and he doubted the fellow would take the impending rejection with the nerveless grace his daughter had. He shot Alex a warning look, hoping the man would have sense enough to find a quieter place to deliver the news than the middle of the ballroom, and excused himself from the conversation. Then he headed across the room to the garden to find Miss Goddard.

He should bring a chaperone, to make this intervention more proper. But was it really necessary?

He did not plan on being outside with her for more than a few moments and might not even have need to speak to her. If she seemed to be in distress, he could turn back and find some matron who might help. If she was not, he would leave her alone and tell no one. That would save her from the embarrassment of his attention.

He did not expect to find what was there, which was nothing. The veranda was empty, as were the benches under the arbours. The rose-bordered paths were clear. No one walked the stepping-stones around the goldfish pond.

It made no sense. He had seen her go out and watched the door as he crossed to it. She had not come back in. Had she climbed back into the house through a window? What purpose would she have had to do it? Was she hiding from her parents?

Having met them, he could hardly blame her. But she had to face them sooner or later. She could not skulk in the garden for ever. He worked his way up and down the paths, peering under bushes, and resisted the urge to call her name. He should go back into the house and trust that she would find her own way in when she was ready. None of this was his business, after all.

It served him right for throwing a party to introduce the players of this little farce. They were headed for a public jilting that would end up in the scandal sheets tomorrow. If he had let the matter resolve without help, fewer people would have known of it. Now, what happened to the girl would be on his head as much as Alex's.

He had reached the end of the last path and followed the perimeter wall at the back. There was no sign of her, to the left or to the right.

Then there was a rustle of leaves and a cry from above, and a dancing slipper struck him in the side of the head, followed by a foot, silken skirts and darkness.

Chapter Three

In her defence, she had tested the ivy before she began to climb, and it had seemed strong enough to hold her. Her mistake had been to pause at the top of the wall to look back the way she had come. She had seen the Duke of Fallon coming down the walk towards her, searching beneath the rosebushes as if he had lost something.

It was curious behaviour and she had wondered at it. More than that, it had given her the excuse to look at him again. It was probably rude to stare. But then, it was also rude to climb the walls of his garden. Once she made her escape, she would never see him again. This would be her last chance to drink in the sight of him and she had best not waste the opportunity.

He was even more handsome in moonlight than he had been in candlelight. The shadows cast by the soft glow made his cheekbones even higher and his fine profile even sharper. She could not help a little sigh as he drew close, walking along the length of the wall towards the place she had climbed.

Had he seen her? It did not seem so. His gaze was fixed forward, and he did not spare a look above him to where she was hanging at the top of the wall. Her fist tightened on the vine, and she felt the shock as it pulled away from the stone in a blanket of leafy green. Her feet slipped from the crack she had wedged them in and suddenly she was jumping for the ground, dragging the ivy down after her.

Fortunately, or unfortunately, the Duke was there to break her fall. For a moment, she was standing on his shoulders. Then her foot slipped, kicking out at his head, and he crumpled to the ground, dazed. She fell with him in a tumble of exposed petticoats and fallen leaves, her bottom hitting the grass with a thump as he rolled to his hands and knees, his face still buried beneath her skirts.

'Oh, dear.'

Her mother was hurrying down the nearest path, her father and the Duke of Glenmoor a few steps behind her.

'What the devil is going on here?' Her father was shouting, which was never good. At the sound of his voice, curious guests crowded in the doorway to the ballroom, trying to catch a glimpse of the scandal that she had created.

She was afraid to look at her father's face, sure that the darkness would not hide the rage that must be brewing in it. Instead, she stared at the hand that the Duke of Glenmoor held out to her as he stepped closer. His other hand was extended to the man on the ground, still stunned and oblivious to what was happening.

When neither of them responded, he sighed and took hold of them anyway, grabbing her hand and the Duke of Fallon's coat collar and pulling them both to their feet with surprising ease. 'Miss Goddard, are you all right?' he said in a tone that was much more patient than she expected or deserved.

'Fine,' she said breathlessly, giving him a nervous smile before looking at the other Duke, who was stammering.

'I d-did not… I do not know how…'

'What the devil do you mean—'

Glenmoor interrupted her father's angry response to the confusion. 'I think it is best that we discuss this in your study, Fallon. Mr Goddard?' He gave a gesture of command that silenced the entire party, then looked to Madeline and her mother. 'Perhaps it would be best for you ladies to compose yourselves in private as well. Ask a footman to show you to the music room.'

Not the ladies' retiring room then. Maddie was in need of it, for she was sure that her skirt was muddy, her stockings torn and leaves still stuck in her carefully coifed hair. But the retiring room would be full of as many female guests as could cram themselves into it, buzzing like bees with speculation about what would happen next.

'The music room,' her mother said with a worried look and a shepherding gesture, and they left behind the men who would decide her fate.

Though Evan was sitting in the chair behind his study desk, the seat that he considered the most powerful in the house, he still felt like a recalcitrant child when he looked at his stepbrother sitting on the other side of the room. Perhaps Alex was growing into his role of Glenmoor, for he had handled the current matter with an aplomb that Evan could not manage. He'd insisted on leaving Mr Goddard in the adjoining library until they could get their story straight enough to form a response to the outraged man.

'I am innocent, I tell you,' Evan announced, resisting the urge to pound the desk with frustration. 'She dropped on me from above like a panther out of a jungle tree.'

Alex was staring at him, every bit the disappointed older brother. 'A panther. I had hoped you would come up with something better than that.'

'I have nothing. I did nothing. I went out into the garden to look for her...'

'Unchaperoned.'

'My first mistake. But I did not mean to talk to her. I just wanted to know she was well.' Because she had not looked like someone able to take care of herself. He had felt sorry for her, since he had thought her an unwilling player in whatever happened tonight. But now he was not so sure. 'I could not find her and was walking along the wall. She must have been climbing the ivy above me.'

'It is a good thing that Goddard is not in the room, for he will never believe that,' Alex said, shaking his head.

'I have nothing else to tell him.'

'You were caught with your head beneath her skirt.' Alex gave a dubious frown.

'It was not intentional.' He tried to forget the feel of silk stocking and equally silky skin against his cheek, for that would do nothing to convince his brother.

'That does not matter,' his brother reminded him. 'You crossed a boundary that no man should breach before marriage, and you were caught by more witnesses than can be sworn to secrecy. It does not matter if the girl is a wall-scaling half-wit, she is now your responsibility. You know what you must do.'

'You expect me to marry her?' he said, still not believing that things had come so far so fast.

'Before this party, you were telling me that she was an excellent prospect,' Alex reminded him.

'For you,' he replied.

'I see.'

'Because of the land.'

'Then you will get the land from Goddard and sell it to me,' Alex said with a contented smile. 'From what her father told me earlier, the deal is even sweeter than you thought. When she's wed, the trust from her grandfather leaves her rich in her own right. She is quite the catch.'

'Then *you* marry her,' Evan snapped with none of the patient encouragement he had offered earlier in the night.

'And get you out of the muddle you have got yourself into?' It was a role he had often forced Alex into when they were younger. It was embarrassing to be reminded of the fact now.

'That is not what I meant.'

'You know you need the money more than I do.' This was said gently but firmly and followed by expectant silence.

'I don't know what you mean,' he lied.

Alex gave him another look of brotherly disappointment. 'It is an open secret about London that your pockets are to let. Though it was kind of you to honour me, I don't know how you raised the money to throw this party.'

It had all been done on credit. Worse yet, it had been done to no purpose, since the match between Alex and Miss Goddard had come to nothing. It seemed he had been caught in the trap he had set. 'I did what I thought was needed,' he said with a shrug.

'And now you must do what is needed again,' Alex said, more gently. 'And you will take the money I give you for the dowry property and the other money Miss Goddard brings with her and make a fresh start with it. This may turn out to be the best possible solution to your problems.'

Anything was possible, Evan supposed. It annoyed him that the solution suggested was both so honourable and so practical. But it embarrassed him that he needed this help at all. After all his father had drummed into him about the duties and deportment of a duke, why could he not manage on his own? 'I was trained to do this,' he said, more to himself than to Alex.

'And I was not,' Alex said with a nod. 'But your upbringing is why I know that, now you are in this strange predicament, you will do the right thing. Honour demands that you marry the girl.'

When they had been students together, Alex had always been able to look at complicated problems and ferret out answers that left Evan puzzled and frustrated. He was just as astute today, cutting through all the nonsense to get to the bones of the dilemma. Honour demanded a wedding.

His father had lectured him from birth on the importance of his good name, and the need to protect it at all costs. If one wanted others' respect, first one must respect oneself. He would not be able to live with himself if he had done something, even inadvertently, that besmirched his reputation, or that of Miss Goddard. The reason for the situation was unimportant. Blaming the girl would not change the outcome.

If he suspected that he had somehow been tricked by her? Then he also had himself to blame for mistaking her wide eyes and too eager smile as a lack of guile. Now, he could rue this underestimation at his leisure for they would have a lifetime to discuss it.

'You have said before that any girl of good breeding would do for a wife,' Alex reminded him.

'When the time came,' Evan added. 'I just did not expect it would happen tonight.'

'Well, it is not as if you are waiting for a love match, are you?' His brother favoured him with a sceptical look.

'Of course not,' he said hurriedly. 'The old Fallon would be rolling in his grave if he thought I'd become so mutton-headed as to make a decision like marriage because of emotion.'

'Then put your pride aside and see reason. One way or another, the girl caught you. She is rich, attractive and of reasonably good family. Marry her and be done with it.'

Evan sighed. When put like that, it did seem to be the logical thing to do. And if his father had taught him nothing else, it was to make his decisions as Duke with cold-blooded expediency. 'Bring the father in and let us make the arrangements. If there is truly no choice to be had, let us get this over with.'

* * *

Men had been going in and out of the Duke's study for an hour. First, it was the two Dukes. Then it was just Fallon and her father. Then, all three together. Surprisingly, there was no shouting, at least none that could be heard from where she waited, peeking out of the music room towards the closed door of the study. At one point she had gathered the nerve to speak and said to her father, 'Perhaps, if I were to apologise...'

She had got no further, quelled to silence with a single dire look from him that said all she needed to know. She'd had far too much input already. Her actions had landed them in the soup. Now, it was up to clearer heads to find a way through it.

When her father reappeared in the study door, he greeted her and her mother with a satisfied sigh. 'It is settled. You will be marrying the Duke of Fallon by special licence, within the week.'

'But I thought...' What had she thought? That her attempted escape had been sufficiently heinous to put her beyond the pale. She would have had to deal with her father's wrath, of course. But even he could not be angry for ever.

At least, she did not think so.

Instead, she was to be married to that blond god.

As if in answer to her thoughts, Fallon appeared, giving a single look in her direction and a sigh before walking past her and down the hall.

She stared after him, tempted to call out, to see if he would return and speak to her, if only for a moment. It did not seem fair that she was engaged for the third time in her short life but had yet to be proposed to. Like the other two betrothals, this one had been arranged by men without a thought or question to what future she might desire for herself.

Then her father came to stand beside her, rocking back on his heels in a posture of total satisfaction. 'It was not what I expected at the beginning of the evening. But with Glenmoor's resistance to the original plan, your own solution has been a godsend. Fallon is not so wealthy, of course. But the title is an old one and well-respected. All in all, I am proud of you, my dear.' Now, he looked to her with a genuine fondness that was both unusual and unexpected.

'I did not plan this,' she said hurriedly. It was always a risk voicing an objection around Father. But perhaps, since he was in a good mood, there would be no repercussions for speaking out. There was no way she could go along letting everyone think that the results of the night had been intentional. 'I was trying to get away.'

Her father's rocking stopped abruptly and he turned to her, all trace of approval vanishing from his expression. 'Running away?'

She had said too much. 'I would not actually have gone anywhere,' she corrected. 'I did not go further than the garden.'

'Well, you will not be doing that again.' His eyes narrowed. 'The husband you are getting is better than you deserve, and I will not let you ruin this. You will be married in a week, if I have to lock you in your room for the whole time to make sure that you cannot spoil the arrangements. Is that clear?'

This time, she did not dare to say more than a soft, 'Yes, Father,' before he led her and her mother to the door.

In the days before the wedding Evan saw nothing of his betrothed and far too much of his future father-in-law. The man found an excuse to visit him almost every day, with some question or other that could have been settled in a letter. Had he procured the licence? Were the preparations for the wedding breakfast satisfactory? Did he prefer salmon over prawns?

The answers were yes, yes and it did not matter. He could feel his temper shortening with each interaction but did his best to hide the fact. It would not make the marriage any easier if he began it entirely sick of his fiancée and her family. He especially did not want to show his temper in front of Alex, if only to prove to his brother that he had been serious in his belief that it didn't matter who one married, as long as the end result favoured the Dukedom.

Above all, he wanted to emulate the previous Duke in that respect and manage his own peerage in the way he had been trained to do. His father had married twice. The first time had been to an earl's daughter to get an heir with a properly august bloodline. The second time had been to a woman who was happy to exchange her inheritance for a title and security. Though there had been no affection in the union, Alex's mother had been an ideal duchess, stylish, sophisticated and popular.

If Evan had managed to combine the two goals in one wedding, he was well on his way to fulfilling his father's wishes. He had researched the family when he had thought that Alex would marry into it. Though Goddard had no title, he had found nothing wrong with the girl's pedigree. If she had been raised with the expectation that she would some day be a duchess, she must have some of the social grace necessary for the job. Since he already had a cheque in his pocket from Alex to cover the cost of the land he would receive in the dowry, there was no question that he would be the richer for marrying the girl.

It was an unusual arrangement to get the money from Alex. But it was less embarrassing than the loan Evan had received from his brother the last time his spending had got ahead of his income. Then, as now, Alex had helped without question, treating him like a beloved, if somewhat irresponsible, younger brother.

But it had always been thus, since their families had combined when they were twelve and ten respectively. Alex had seen from the first that Evan had no head for figures and had coached him through lessons and cheated for him when Evan could not seem to complete even the most remedial calculations. Things had not changed when they had grown and Evan was entrusted with the books to the Fallon estate.

It was embarrassing to admit that, after all the training his father had put him through to prepare him to take the coronet, he was still an idiot when it came to managing the money.

Evan glanced at his brother, who was now beside him at the altar of St George's, ready to stand witness at his marriage, searching for the words to thank him for the help he had given. 'You know that the amount you paid me for the Goddard land was wildly inflated.'

'It includes my wedding gift,' Alex replied, staring out over a church that was surprisingly full given the brief time allotted to arrange things. He cocked his head towards the crowd. 'Did your father-in-law organise this?'

'He is not that for a few more minutes,' Evan corrected. 'And yes. He thinks to win the grace of the *ton* with vulgar display.'

Alex smiled. 'Good luck to him on that. And to you as well, for you shall have him camping on your doorstep once the parson has tied the knot.'

'Then he will find that some things cannot be bought, and my favour is one of them,' Evan replied, glancing at the doorway, where the Goddard family had appeared. Perhaps he was not the only one feeling apprehensive of the future today. As Miss Goddard was escorted down the aisle towards him, ready to plight her troth, she looked…

He stared at her, trying to decide what that unusual expression on her face meant. Terror, he decided. She was as frightened of this as he was. But if that was how she felt, then she should not have orchestrated the incident in the garden.

He could feel his mouth setting in a grim line.

In response, she seemed to shrink from his displeasure.

He took a deep breath, let it out in a sigh and relaxed his face. It would do no good to frighten her further. If they must be married, then he must do his best to make the wedding unremarkable and the union passably content.

His father had assured him that marriage need not be that different from being single. He need not associate with his wife if he did not wish to. Nor would he have to change his social life to suit her. He had proven so in his second marriage, spending as little time with Alex's mother as he could after the wedding, leaving her to her interests while he kept to his.

Of course, his father had already had an heir at that point. At least for a time, Evan would need to show much more than superficial interest in his new bride.

But the time they spent together would be no hardship. She was a lovely girl with a trim figure. Her movements were graceful, or at least they were when she was not falling on him from above. The thought made him smile and he directed it to her, silently encouraging her as she made her way to his side.

A responding smile flickered on her lips for only a moment. Then her face returned to the same worried expression she had worn at the church door. She stood quietly as the bishop began the ceremony, reciting her part of the vows in a barely audible whisper.

He said his part as well, in a clear voice, hoping his volume could counter her lack. And when the moment came for him to kiss the bride, he leaned down and offered a buss on lips that were formed in a sweet 'O' of surprise.

It was nice.

There was no place for passion when standing before the altar. He should not even think about where kissing might lead. But perhaps it would not be so bad to be married to Madeline Goddard. Tonight, he might find it quite enjoyable.

From the church, they went to the room that Goddard had hired for the breakfast. Once there, though the celebration around them was raucous, his new wife was even more quiet than she had been in the church, accepting the food offered her with a polite nod and pushing it about her plate without eating.

The people around them took no notice of her silence, for her father overfilled any conversational gaps. He seemed to go on and on, pontificating about nothing, blissfully unaware of the ass he was making of himself. Alex, who was seated beside the fellow, was doing his best to get a word in, probably relieved that, in the future, Goddard would not be his cross to bear.

That would fall to Evan. But not today. Today, he could ignore the man and play the dutiful husband with eyes only for his bride.

He glanced at the woman at his side again and thought of the night to come. She was innocent, he was sure. Experienced flirts had a certain air about them, and she had nothing of the kind. Instead of casting glances at him from beneath lowered lids, she kept her eyes fixed on her plate. Her cheeks wore a flush of pink that had more to do with her reaction to her father's embarrassing behaviour than any application of rouge.

She would be unskilled but sweet and cooperative. In turn, he would be slow and gentle. Hopefully, her mother had explained her duties to her so his actions would not come as too big a shock. But in the end… At last…

He gave her an encouraging smile, thinking about the satisfaction to come.

She sensed his attention and looked up at him, blinking her wide green eyes slowly, as if she did not understand the reason for his interest. Then she looked away again, moving her fork as if it weighed several stone and lifting a bite of salmon slowly to her mouth, chewing equally slowly, waiting for him to lose interest again and go back to his meal.

Maddie chewed her food, which seemed to have no flavour at all, trying to come to terms with the way her life had changed in a few short days. The Duke was just as handsome in daylight as he had been in candlelight. Dazzlingly so. She felt like a mud hen, sitting in the bright sunlight of his smile. When they were seen together in public, people would remark on the difference between them and wonder why he had not chosen a prettier girl.

She took a deep sip of champagne and felt the bubbles going straight to her head. He was probably as intelligent as he was handsome. What would she ever have to say to such a man? Of course, if he was anything like her father, he would not want to converse with her. She glanced down the table, wishing that he had a sister or mother or some other female relative with whom she could keep company when she went to her new home. But the only family her husband had was his brother, the Duke, who was sitting beside her father.

Their eyes met and he offered her a smile and saluted with his glass, as if they were sharing a secret toast. She took another drink. It was a shame that the match between them had not worked out, for Glenmoor seemed to be a kind man and far less intimidating than her new husband.

Of course, when she looked at Glenmoor, she did not feel the strange, fluttery nervousness of body and spirit that she felt when she thought of her husband. But perhaps it would have been easier to wed a man who was not quite so exciting.

The breakfast was ending, and her plate was still mostly full, but her stomach was so unsteady she did not trust herself to take more than a few bites of anything. The previous evening, her mother had come into her room and explained in embarrassing detail what would be expected of her on her wedding night. It had all seemed highly improbable, like a story made up to frighten virgins into good behaviour.

But her mother had insisted that it was true, and that, from start to finish, it would not take very long, and the lights would be out the whole time.

She took another drink, which steadied her nerves but made the rest of her feel decidedly unsteady, as she rose from the table.

As if sensing her need for support, her new husband took her by the arm and escorted her out of the room towards a carriage with an impressive green crest on the door. His family coat of arms, she assumed, squinting in the sun at the lettering above the shield.

Fallon nodded as if approving her interest. *"'Nil moror ictus",'* he repeated for her. 'It means "I heed not blows."'

She tipped her head to the side, considering. His response meant two things. The first was that, if he did not heed them, he had probably never been hit hard enough to make a difference in his behaviour.

The other was that he did not think she could read Latin. She had no right to be disappointed by his underestimation of her learning. It might not be a common skill amongst girls. She had learned it more out of boredom than need. If he enjoyed proving that he was smarter than her in something, he might be no different than her father, and she should probably let the matter pass without comment.

So she replied with an, 'Oh,' in a tone that thanked him for his clarification, and allowed him to help her into the carriage. The press of his hand at her elbow was unexpectedly intimate, unsettling her nerves again. When he withdrew, she could not decide whether to be relieved or disappointed.

He took a seat across the carriage so that he might look at her, which was even more unnerving. Now that they were alone, the full force of his interest was directed to her. What was he thinking? More importantly, what did he think of her?

Then he spoke again. 'In the garden at the ball, just what was it you were doing up on the wall? Did you intend to drop down on me as you did?'

She did her best to hide her disappointment at the question, which answered hers all too well. He thought she'd entrapped him. She should not have been surprised. A man as important as he was would assume everything was about him. She resisted the urge to roll her eyes, for it would likely not end well for her. 'I was birdwatching,' she said, staring back at him and waiting for his response.

'At night?' He raised an eyebrow.

'For owls,' she added.

'I see.' He frowned and she immediately regretted her glib response. 'And will there be any more of this behaviour in the future?'

'No,' she said, wondering if it was the truth. Though she had considered running away before that night, it had been the sudden cancellation of her engagement that had decided her. She had not known what she wanted, but she had been sure she had not wanted to go home and face her father's wrath. But now?

She had no idea what kind of a man her new husband was. She gave him a nervous smile.

He replied with a satisfied nod. And then the conversation ended. A short time later, they arrived at the same house she had tried to run from less than a week ago, and she was escorted across the threshold to meet the assembled staff.

'And this is Mrs Miller,' Fallon announced, leading her up to the housekeeper that waited at the head of the row. 'She will give you a tour of the house and show you to your rooms.' He favoured them both with a brilliant smile, and bowed deeply to Maddie, as if there was a real honour in having been forced to marry her. 'And now, if you will excuse me, I have business to attend to.' Then he turned and walked down the hall that she knew led to his study.

She stared after him, wishing he could spare a few more minutes of his time so she might talk with him, to get to know him better before the inevitable night that would follow this day. But since she could hardly find the nerve to speak in his presence, it would be a waste of his valuable time.

As the housekeeper walked her through the ground floor, her mind raced ahead to the bedrooms and what she assumed would happen in the evening. The thought of doing the things her mother had described with a stranger was inconceivable. She had not even known Fallon's full name until this morning. If he did not mean to spend any time with her this afternoon, she might learn nothing more about him until the candles were out and they were fumbling around in the dark.

As they walked up the stairs to the family wing, she considered the main doors just behind her and wondered what the woman next to her would think if she turned and ran, again. She had not thought things could get worse than they had been living with her short-tempered father. But today she felt even smaller and more miserable than she had at home.

'And here are the keys.'

'I beg your pardon?' Her attention snapped back to the present and the housekeeper, who had produced a key ring from her apron pocket.

Mrs Miller was staring at her in sympathy, as if she realised how overwhelming this day must be for her. 'The keys to your room. There is a set for the rest of the house as well, but it is rather bulky. His Grace's mother left them to me and only called for them when she needed them.'

'I see.' She stared at the things being offered to her in amazement. She had been locked in rooms and locked out of them. But never in her life had she been offered the chance to come and go as she pleased. Maddie reached out and took the pair of iron keys, fitting one of them into the lock of the room in front of them.

The door swung open on well-oiled hinges and the housekeeper announced, 'It is not the height of fashion, of course. Nothing has been done to it since the mistress passed. But it is clean and aired and the linens have been changed for you. Your maid has already unpacked your things.'

'It is charming,' Maddie assured her, relieved to see that it was. The walls were covered in rose silk and there was an upholstered bench by the window that would be perfect for reading.

There was also a door on the side wall that she suspected would lead to the Duke's room. She ran her finger over the second key in her hand and walked to the door to test her theory.

'It is already unlocked,' the housekeeper announced, as if this was in any way reassuring.

Maddie opened it and stared into a room as masculine as hers was feminine. She shut it quickly again.

'Yes, well, then…' She took a deep breath and yet it still did not seem to fill her lungs. It felt as if she was under water and the next breath in would be the one to drown her. She gripped the doorway for support and looked helplessly back at the housekeeper.

'I expect this is all very sudden for you, Your Grace,' she said with a motherly smile. 'A new marriage and a large house, all at the same time.'

Maddie managed a weak nod in response.

'Why don't you rest here for a while? I will have tea sent up to you.'

'That would be nice.' At the thought of a moment's quiet, she was able to breathe again. She squeezed the keys in her hand so tight that she felt the metal marking her palm. She must remember that, as long as she was here, she was safe. So she smiled back at the housekeeper, who went off to get the tea.

As soon as she was gone, Maddie locked the doors.

Chapter Four

That night, when Evan came down to dinner, he found himself alone at the table. It was most unexpected, since he had assumed that his new wife would be eager for the splendid meal that the cook had prepared to showcase her culinary talents for the new mistress of the house.

But when he enquired after her, he was informed by the servants that she had taken ill and requested a tray in her room.

It was ridiculous. There had been nothing wrong with her that morning. She had been a little pale, perhaps. And quiet. But she had always been thus around him, so that was no surprise. She had been quiet in her room as well, for he had been just next door to her as he'd dressed for dinner and had not heard a peep from her side of the shared wall. She'd had several hours to rest since the wedding. If she was still in bed at dinner, it was nothing more than malingering, and he would tell her so.

He threw his napkin aside, went up the stairs to her room and knocked sharply on the door. 'Madeline, are you in there?'

'No. I mean, yes. But I am not well.' The words came hesitantly, as if she'd had trouble forming them. Was she truly in some sort of distress?

He tried the door and found it locked. 'Let me in.'

'No.' This was delivered in a firm tone, as if she had finally found her nerve.

He raised his fist to hammer on the door and demand that she open it, then stopped himself. A display of temper would be an embarrassment in front of the servants, nor did it set the best tone for the first day of his marriage. But neither could he allow her to bar the door to him without at least offering an explanation.

So he turned away and went into his own room, snatched the key from the dresser and opened the connecting door, which was locked, just as he'd expected it to be.

She was sitting on the edge of her bed, skin pale against the blush pink of the same gown she had worn to the church. Her hands, which were clasped in her lap, seemed even whiter, each tendon outlined by the stress of her grip, as if she was hanging on to an invisible lifeline that tethered her to the earth. As he stepped over the threshold to go to her, he saw her flinch.

'You were not thinking clearly if you did not realise that I had a key to this door as well,' he said softly, and she flinched again.

'How stupid of me.' The words were barely audible, as if she said them to herself and not him.

'What is the meaning of this nonsense?' he asked, waving at the locked door.

For a moment she went silent again. Then she took a deep breath as if she needed it to force the words out. 'I just… I do not think I can do this.'

'Do what?' he said, honestly confused.

'The marriage. All of it.' She made a brief upward gesture with her hands, then clasped them hurriedly again.

'It is a bit late to decide that now,' he replied, allowing himself a short, bitter laugh. 'You might have some childish idea about an annulment, but they are damned hard to get, even if I would permit one.' But wasn't that secretly what he wanted as well? To start the week over so that he could have avoided the mishap that had led to this marriage. Despite what he'd been telling himself, to marry was to lose one's freedom. It was all too much, too soon.

He raised his hand to run harried fingers through his hair and she flinched again, turning her head as if bracing for a blow.

He lowered his arm slowly, watching her.

She let out the breath she'd been holding and coloured, as if embarrassed by her involuntary response.

He felt his own blood heat with rage and disgust. He had never given any woman a reason to cower at his temper. What had Goddard done to this one to leave her so easily frightened?

When next he spoke, he made sure his voice was soft and calm, giving no reason to cause alarm. 'When we met in the garden, what were you really doing? And no fustian this time about watching for owls.'

'I was trying to run away,' she said in a small voice. 'Glenmoor did not want me, and I did not dare tell my father that.'

'I see.' And how did he not notice before? When she had been reticent, he had thought her simple, or perhaps only shy. But she had been terrified, of him and every other man who had been a part of her life.

'And what did you want? Did you want to marry Glenmoor?'

She shook her head. 'It did not really matter because I was not consulted. Not about him, or the man before him. Or you,' she added, staring down at the floor in embarrassment.

He should not have been surprised by the rejection. She had locked the door against him, after all. But he was unaccustomed to being refused. He was powerful. Though it was immodest to agree, he had been told that he was handsome. And though he was not precisely rich, he wore his debt like a bespoke jacket, making it seem stylish and desirable. Against all logic, women adored him for it.

Without thinking, he sat down on the bed next to her and felt her shrink away from him. 'You needn't worry,' he said in a gentle voice. 'I am not going to make matters worse by demanding affection that you are not prepared to give. But neither can I just send you back to your parents and pretend that this marriage did not happen.'

Her head jerked up in alarm and the expression on her face said that she dreaded the possibility of that even more than she did his presence in her bedroom.

'But I think, as two reasonable people...' He

looked at her closely. 'You are reasonable, I hope. And I consider myself to be so.' He waited for her hesitant nod of agreement. 'We should be able to find some way to muddle through this together. There are advantages to marriage, after all…' Though damned if he could think of what they might be at the moment.

She nodded with slightly more enthusiasm. 'Peace and stability.'

'A tranquil home,' he said, trying not to think of his father and stepmother and their tendency to rage at each other and slam doors on the rare times they shared the house.

'Children,' she said, biting her lip as if she dreaded to suggest them.

'Perhaps not immediately,' he replied gently. 'It might be better if we got to know each other first.'

She seemed to relax at this and offered him a hesitant smile. 'I think I would like that.'

His own reaction to the words surprised him. Was the room uncomfortably warm, or was he flushing at the thought of the exploration before them that would inevitably lead to the marriage bed? He had not seen much value in courtship until this moment. But then, he had never been with a girl who had refused him.

He smiled back at her, feeling strangely pleased with the unexpected turn the day had taken. 'I think I would like it as well. But for now, I think I would like some dinner. Would you accompany me, Your Grace?'

'Yes. And thank you, Your Grace.' Then she took the hand he offered and allowed him to lead her down to the dining room.

Maddie woke the next morning from a deep, dreamless sleep between heavy linen sheets scented with lavender. After the Duke had taken her down to dinner, he had gone out of his way to be gentle to her, and spoken of trivialities to pass the time, encouraging her to enjoy their meal.

For her part, she had eaten little, and responded eagerly when he had suggested that it had been a trying day and that they make an early night of it. Then he had escorted her back to her room, releasing her with a soft squeeze of her fingers and the exhortation to sleep well.

And he had never raised a hand to her.

It was not until she was alone in her room again that she realised how tense she had been, and how expectant for the slap that did not come. She was guilty of a betrayal of biblical proportions by refusing her husband on their wedding night. Such disobedience could not go unpunished. Could it?

Apparently, it could, for the right kind of man. She could not help the little smile playing across her lips as she thought of him, handsome, patient and understanding. If she had not thought him the perfect man before, now that she was getting to know him, she was convinced.

She went to the window and looked out on the morning, which was bright and fresh, just the sort of new beginning she was hoping for in her life. And there, below her, was the garden that had been her undoing. Or perhaps it had been the making of the new her. It was too soon to tell.

Either way, she could not help the desire to go down and walk amongst the flowers again. She called for her maid, dressed and went down the stairs and out of the ballroom doors, and down the path.

The roses were as fresh and sweet as the morning, in all stages from bud to full-blown, and dotted with crystal droplets of dew. She bent down to smell them, closing her eyes and taking the scent deep into her lungs, letting it wash away the fears of yesterday. Then she proceeded down the path, which ended at the patch of wall that had been denuded of its ivy covering by her fall.

'If you are thinking of climbing again, it would be best if we got you a ladder.'

The voice took her by surprise, and she spun around to see the Duke coming down the path towards her, approaching so silently that he was almost upon her before she had heard him.

He went on. 'Or you could go to the kitchen gardens and try climbing the grape arbour. Those vines are sturdier than the ivy.'

He was joking with her, and she tried to respond in kind. 'In my defence, I tested it before I began. It seemed strong enough.'

'You needn't have run, you know. The ruined engagement was none of your doing,' the Duke said, laying a reassuring hand on her arm. 'Alex was adamant that he would not be married, even before he spoke to you. I tried to convince him that it was all for the best, but he would not have it.'

'It would not have mattered,' she said with a sigh. 'Someone must be blamed for the failure. And Father could not very well have shouted at the Duke.'

Her own duke blinked at her in understanding. 'And where did you mean to go?'

'My former governess,' she said, realising how

silly the plan must sound in the light of day. 'I had hoped that she would help me find a position as a governess or schoolteacher.'

'A teacher,' he repeated, as if the idea surprised him. 'Then you really were not trying to catch me unawares.'

'Certainly not,' she assured him. 'I had no idea that you would be there.' Had he thought that she'd meant to force a marriage to the first available man? She hesitated, then added, 'My father might tell you something quite different, however. He wanted to see me married to a man with a title, and to him one duke is quite like another.'

He gave her a lopsided smile that was even more charming than his normal ones. 'Well, that is good to know, at least. It is important that we start our marriage with no secrets between us.'

'And I did not mean to interrupt your walk today either,' she added. 'I just saw the garden from my window…'

'And you could not resist,' he finished for her. 'It is quite all right. There is more than enough room here for us both to enjoy. And do not be shy if you wish to cut blooms to take into the house. I admit that I am quite fond of having roses in the common rooms.' He reached out to touch a peach-coloured blossom.

She stared at his hand, admiring the long fingers and neatly trimmed nails. He was so gentle with the flower that the petals barely moved as he stroked them. Would he touch her the same way, when they were alone together? The thought made her shiver with something that was not quite fear.

'I assume you are skilled at arranging flowers,' he said, dragging his nail along the edge of a petal, then lowering his head to inhale its fragrance.

She was not. She preferred her flowers to be alive on the stem like this one was. But if cut roses made him happy, she would provide them. 'The next time I come out, I will bring scissors,' she said, still staring dazedly at his hand.

He turned from the flower and offered her his arm. 'And now, may I escort you in to breakfast? You must be quite hungry, after yesterday.'

It was probably true. She had barely eaten yesterday. She should be near to starving. But at the moment, all she could think about was the feel of his coat sleeve as she slipped her hand into the crook of his elbow. 'Breakfast would be nice,' she agreed. Not as nice as walking arm-in-arm with him, but nice all the same.

Chapter Five

Evan was relieved to see that much progress had been made in a single day of marriage. His wife was eating her breakfast today, rather than pushing it around the plate. Nor had she tried to run away from him during the night or this morning in the garden. Instead, they'd had a civil conversation, a distinct improvement on last night's dinner, where he had talked and she'd sat mute.

She liked the garden. The fact made him smile, for it was a sign of common ground between them. He prized his roses and had a staff of gardeners in country and city to care for them.

Of course, in a normal marriage he would not be considering trivialities this morning. If he had married someone else, he would have been rising late after initiating his bride into the arts of love, and not celebrating every word that he could pry out of her mouth.

But the happy union would happen in time, he was sure. And the anticipation would sweeten the act and make it more enjoyable for both of them. The old Duke would have found such concern over the girl's pleasure to be unnatural. But Evan had begun to remember what it was like the rare times his father and stepmother had shared the house, the long awkward silences and sudden bouts of tears or shouting.

Such arguments had been unpleasant for Alex and him and he had no desire to repeat them in his own marriage. For the sake of his future children, it would be better to find some harmony with their mother before demanding immediate and passionate relief.

He allowed himself a moment to imagine their joining, surprised at the rush of heat as he pictured her, accepting and unafraid, smiling up at him in the afterglow.

Perhaps she was having similar thoughts. Or perhaps he had missed something while fantasising about her. At the moment, she was sitting across the breakfast table from him with an expectant look on her face, as if she had already asked a question and was awaiting the answer.

For the life of him, he could not think of what it could be that she wanted from him. He had spent all morning with her thus far. But he could not stay here all day and get to know her better. He had a session of parliament and meant to visit his club after. No matter how necessary, further socialising with Madeline would have to wait. 'I must be going,' he said, tossing his napkin beside his empty plate. 'And I expect you have things to do as well.' A goodbye kiss would be appropriate once he knew her better. It would be pleasant as well. But he did not want to frighten her, so he settled for a smile and a nod of farewell, then waited for a similar gesture from her.

Instead, she gave him a quizzical smile. 'That is just it,' she said. 'What is the rest of my day? I was wondering what my duties might be.'

'Duties,' he said, surprised.

'As your wife.' She wet her lips. 'Other than…' She paused again, clearly not wanting to mention the thing they had omitted last night. 'You have parliament, of course. And I assume you have a club that you will visit, and other things that will keep you busy and away from home.'

He smiled again, pleased to see that she understood him so perfectly. It was another auspicious sign.

But there was that expectant look again. 'And what might you wish me to do with my days?'

'I have no opinion on the matter,' he said, easing back into his chair. 'Run the house, I suppose.'

'Great houses often have systems in place that it is better not to tamper with,' she said, blinking at him. 'I would not want to be making improvements that hinder the running of things. And I certainly do not want to alter something without your permission, only to find that you particularly liked it.'

'Of course not,' he said, hoping she did not mean to consult him in every decision she made.

'I was wondering if there is anything you wish me to do. Are there things you want me to change? Or activities you wish me to participate in?'

'When we are in the country, perhaps,' he said. 'There, there are tenants to visit. And they always seem to have a sick aunt or a new baby, or something that should be seen to. But in London?' He shrugged and helped himself to a final rasher of bacon, chewing to give himself time to think. 'There will be parties and balls to attend. We are here to be seen, after all. You will need clothes appropriate for all sorts of functions.'

'Other than the clothes I have?' she said, surprised.

He scanned what she was wearing, which was functional, he supposed. But not nearly as opulent as his stepmother had worn, even when she was not leaving the house. 'Your current wardrobe is suitable for life in the country, and for an unmarried girl. But duchesses dress differently.' He had no idea how to explain said difference. All gowns looked pretty much alike to him. But women seemed to have strong opinions and to judge each other based on what they were wearing. He did not want her to be found wanting by her peers. 'You are as much a symbol of the house of Fallon as I am and I expect you to be in the first stare of fashion.'

'You expect me to shop?' she said, looking confused.

'Yes,' he said, wondering where he would find the money to kit out a female in a suitable manner. 'You will do quite a bit of that while in London.' It was something women liked, after all. Then he brightened. 'And I shall expect you to entertain.'

'You have just had a ball,' she reminded him.

And a damn bother it had been, even though he had left the planning of it to the staff.

'A dinner?' she suggested.

'That will be sufficient to start on,' he replied, relieved that she had thought of something to fill the gap in her time. 'Have Mrs Miller find the guest list of the last dinner I went to and emulate that.'

'And beyond that?'

'Whatever you like,' he said with an expansive gesture. 'Make calls on your friends. Pursue hobbies. Painting watercolours or embroidering screens, or whatever it is that you like to do.'

'I see,' she said, and he thought, for a moment, she looked quite grim. Then she offered what was obviously a forced smile. 'I will find a hobby.'

'Yes,' he said with a smile, then added, 'Do you like horses? Riding, perhaps?'

'Not really.' Her face fell. 'And I have never handled a carriage.'

'That is good.' He seized on another similarity between them. 'Though I would get you one if you wanted it, I do not keep riding horses in the city, and the Fallon carriage has drivers and grooms.'

'I see.'

'Do you play the pianoforte?' he asked. 'Because sometimes music is nice, of an evening.'

'No,' she said, looking remorseful.

'Well, I do,' he said with a shrug. 'Not that there is much reason for it. I can keep up with the best of the young ladies on display in the season, if I wish to.'

'Did you have a music teacher?' she asked, surprised.

He shook his head again. 'I taught myself. I do not think my father found it seemly, since it did not really have anything to do with the running of the estate, but he did not forbid it.' Then he looked at her, considering. 'For you, however, I will hire a music master.'

'Thank you,' she replied with an expression that said she was unsure of whether she was grateful or not.

'Other than that, you can choose your own daytime activities.' He wasn't just running out of ideas, he was completely without further suggestions for her. What did women do during the day?

'I'll just keep busy, shall I?' she said in a bright tone that was definitely false.

'That would be best,' he agreed, relieved that the conversation was at an end. 'I will be home for supper. We will discuss it again then.'

But he hoped they would not.

* * *

For the sake of the servants Maddie maintained her smile as she finished her breakfast, but her mind was working furiously, trying to decide what to make of the information she'd been given.

Apparently, her husband knew even less about her future than she did. She could not exactly make calls on London friends until she made some, having left her few friends in the country to marry a duke. And as far as hobbies went?

She had one, but he had not listed it. Apparently, he imagined a wife, as delicate as the roses he grew, dressing in frills and arranging flowers and then painting pictures of those flowers, with the process being repeated endlessly, until the house was full of dead blooms and mediocre art.

It was not as bad as the life she'd led in her father's house, where she'd been afraid to speak or to act. But the days described just now sounded dull beyond words and not at all like her.

She could not really blame the Duke for not understanding her true nature, since she'd made an effort to keep it a secret, so as not to disappoint him. But she did not want to be an ornament. She was a thinking human being.

And it seemed that men seldom anticipated the

sort of woman that had rational thoughts, nor knew what to do with one when they had one. Her father had much preferred that she spend her time hemming handkerchiefs and knitting socks rather than working proofs or solving equations. He thought her interest in mathematics unladylike and took her textbooks from her whenever he saw them, fearing that she would end her days as an unmarriageable bluestocking.

And now it seemed that her new husband might think the same way. Nothing he had said to her just now had encouraged her to improve her mind. Perhaps what her father said was true, and men did not want women who might challenge them in any way.

She would introduce her interests to him slowly to see how he reacted. Perhaps a watercolour for each afternoon spent in calculation, and a flower arrangement before each mathematics lecture she attended, and he would remain convinced that she was the sort of pretty and useless wife he had hoped for.

For now, she took scissors out into the rose garden and apologised silently as she cut some of the best blooms for the house. She called for vases and arranged them in the morning room, in the dining room, and, as an afterthought, she chose the best bloom of them all and put it in a crystal bowl for her husband's study.

When she went to the room, the door was open, so she slipped in, meaning to set the bowl on the desk and go. But there, laid out across the surface, were the account books for the estate.

Accounting. It was just another form of mathematics, and it made her smile that there was another interest she might share with her husband. These books were a major part of his life.

And they were in his private study.

Maddie looked at the open door, where at any moment a servant might appear. She had not been forbidden from this room, but she doubted that the Duke would want her tarrying here without his knowledge. Perhaps, when he knew her better, she could ask permission to see the ledgers, so she might find ways to help him with small economies in the housekeeping.

Or she could look quickly now. Just a peek to satisfy her curiosity. She glanced at the door again and opened the top ledger, just a crack. And then full open on the desk.

It was amazing. In the first book, which seemed to cover the London house, there were pages and pages of expenses for this month alone. Wages for a staff of twenty, deliveries of the food to feed them all, cases of wine for the cellar, some things paid, and others carried over until next month, and some carried over from the month before. And then, tucked into the back cover, were the bills received that had not yet been entered, along with IOUs, scribbled notes and other flotsam that had probably come from her husband's coat pockets. Filed haphazardly amongst them was their wedding licence, and the notation that the bishop had been given the princely sum of ten pounds for performing the ceremony.

Without thinking, she slid into her husband's big leather chair and settled in to read, amazed at the amount of money that changed hands in an average month, just to keep life running smoothly, silently and with no apparent effort for the people who lived above stairs.

She was also surprised by the numbers of blots and cross-outs on the many lines before her. On the desk to the side, there was a stack of writing paper with several pages of equally messy calculations and abortive efforts to make the various entries total properly. Her palms itched at the sight of those mistakes, which could be set right with a little time and patience. She had the time, far too much of it, in fact, and her husband had so little. And she had not just patience, she had initiative and ability.

She probably shouldn't. But could doing something so useful truly be bad?

She sharpened a quill and got to work.

As it always did when she had figures before her, time seemed to slow and her mind focused on the equations, blotting out all outside interruptions. The maths was hardly challenging, simple addition and subtraction, but it gave her a sense of comfort to see the lines come out right, and the neat columns of figures where there had been numerical anarchy before. The world had order again. The future that had been unknown was secure.

'What are you doing?'

She started with surprise, leaping up out of the chair. Though no time at all seemed to have passed, the clock was striking three. She had missed lunch and her husband was standing in the doorway, staring at her in horror.

She dropped the quill she had been holding, which made a fresh blot on the ledger. 'I was just totalling the last line.'

'Of what?' he said, though it ought to have been clear that she was referring to the books in front of her. The question was rhetorical, and she had no good answer to explain why she was sitting here.

'I brought you a flower,' she said. It was hardly a sop to make up for what she had done afterwards, but what could she say? 'And since I was in the room already, I noticed that the accounts needed balancing.'

'In a closed ledger on a desk that does not belong to you,' he said, folding his arms and looking nothing like the agreeable man she had shared breakfast with.

So she said nothing, just waited in growing terror for the explosion she was sure would come.

'And what made you think that I wanted your help?'

A part of her was tempted to announce that it was clear, by the mistakes in the books, that someone's help was needed. But then she remembered her place and apologised instead. 'I overstepped myself.'

'Did you.' Again, it was a statement rather than a question.

Stupid girl. Stupid, stupid girl.

The words she'd heard so often from her father echoed in her head. Why had she meddled? Why wasn't she the sort of girl that anyone wanted?

'I just wanted to look,' she said, closing her eyes against the glare on her husband's perfect face. 'And I noticed a small error. Minuscule, in the scheme of things. But when I saw it, I could not help but track it down.'

'You could not help yourself,' he said, voice dripping with sarcasm.

She opened her eyes and stepped away from the desk, backing towards the window. 'It will not happen again.'

'See that it doesn't,' he said, taking his rightful place behind the desk and closing the book with a slam as she backed towards the door. 'You have your duties, and I have mine. And yours do not involve bookkeeping.'

'Of course not, Your Grace,' she said, and ran from the room before she embarrassed herself by crying.

Now that he was alone, Evan approached the desk and the ledger on it with the typical dread he felt whenever he had to deal with it. She had described what he had done so far as a minuscule error, which they both knew was a whopping great lie. She had seen the mess he had made of the books and, worse yet, she had been able to understand and fix his mistakes.

He pushed the books aside, stopping just short of dumping them onto the floor in a rage. After all the time and training he'd had in the running of the estate, he should not still have made mistakes. Normally, he avoided them by letting his man of business, Ramsey, take care of the accounting, but he'd decided that it was time to make an effort and prove to himself that he was capable of handling things.

And, as always happened when he was faced with doing calculations, the numbers would not seem to behave for him. It was as if they danced out of the way when he tried to focus on them, purposely refusing to line up in columns like soldiers and allow themselves to be counted.

His wife seemed to have no such problem. She had seen nothing but opportunity in the unfinished work, and fun and games in correcting the errors he had made.

He stared down at what she had done, and it seemed right. The totals balanced at the bottom, just as they should. If a slip of a country girl could manage this, why couldn't he? And what did she think of his lack of skill in a thing that came so easily to her?

He laughed bitterly to himself. She was too frightened to think of anything. She was likely upstairs, expecting a beating for her impertinence. Or maybe that he would send her to bed without supper, as one would a disobedient child.

Things had been going so well. She had started to talk to him, to open to him like the rose on his desk. But he had seen her smiling over his greatest shame and had not been able to stop himself from snapping at her. He had frightened her again and they would likely be going back to the awkwardness of yesterday.

John Ramsey appeared in the doorway, knocking politely on the door-frame to request entrance.

'What?' Evan demanded, not bothering to hide his annoyance.

'I noticed you had returned early and was wondering if you had finished with the books, or if, perhaps, you needed my help.' The man did not mean to sound patronising. No one would dare to patronise a duke. But Evan heard it in his question, all the same.

'No, I do not need help,' he said, pushing the finished totals across the desk for his man of business to see. 'They are all in order.'

Ramsey looked down at the ledgers and blinked

twice in rapid succession. It was the only sign of his surprise. 'I see. They are just as they should be. Very good.'

Did he recognise the change in handwriting? There was nothing distinctly feminine about the formation of the numbers, but there was a confidence in her pen strokes that was lacking when he attempted to total the lines.

Ramsey had been managing the estate since his father was Duke, and had seen his fumblings before. He would see the difference and he would know that Evan had received help. How disappointed he must be at the way Evan was running things in comparison to his father. Where there had been wealth, now there was debt, and he could not seem to sort out the reason for it on his own. But today, at least, there was no problem.

'Do you wish to do the same next month?' Ramsey said, one part curiosity, one part pity.

'Of course,' he lied. He wanted nothing of the sort. He never wanted to see the damned things again. But to admit defeat and turn it all over to the other man was even more shameful than struggling with them. He wanted to believe that with enough attempts, if he could not master them, he would at least be able to read the numbers.

'Very well,' said Ramsey, his expression full of doubt.

It galled. He should look confident. It was what he was paid to do. Evan gave him a level stare and announced, 'I will look over the books every month, just as I always have.'

And then Ramsey would correct his mistakes and say nothing about it, just as he always did. The unspoken agreement between them would continue and today would be nothing more than an aberration. Ramsey nodded.

'I thank you for your patience in these matters,' Evan grumbled, and ran a hand through his hair, creating disorder so that he might have an excuse to smooth it again. Then he began to sort the other papers on his desk so he did not have to meet the other man's gaze. 'For your skill and discretion in dealing with the finances, please give yourself a ten percent rise in salary.'

'Thank you, Your Grace,' the man said, and a grateful smile wiped away any earlier doubts.

'You are dismissed, Ramsey.'

'Thank you again.' The man hurried from the study with the light step of a man trying to decide how he would spend his extra funds.

At his absence, Evan slumped in his desk chair,

relieved. There was one matter settled. Now, he must find a way to deal with his wife.

Upstairs in her room, Maddie sat on the edge of her bed, hands clasped in a wasted gesture of penance. Her husband was not there to see how sorry she was, nor did she think she could convey in words how foolish she felt for letting the time get away from her and allowing herself to be caught in his study.

It was not as if she could have hidden her intervention in his accounting. She had not been able to stop once she had started, and the changes she had made to his figures had been significant. But she had hoped that there would be time to explain, before he had discovered them.

Then she could tell him gently of the near obsession she felt when faced with equations that did not balance. She could not help but right them.

Of course, if she had not meddled in his affairs, she would not have noticed the problem. It had been rather like correcting him in his own job, and she should have known better than to contradict a man.

But he had seemed so different from her father that for a moment—no, a few hours—she had forgotten what she was trained to be. He had all but stated that he wanted her to keep to her knitting, or painting, or whatever female occupation he imagined her in.

She had agreed. And then she had gone and spoiled everything by being herself.

There was a knock on the door and she held her breath, afraid to answer. Then her husband's voice came through the oak panel. 'Madeline, may I come in, please?'

'Of course, Your Grace,' she said automatically, unclasping her hands to smooth her hair and hoping she did not look like a red-faced, tantrum-prone child.

When he entered, it was obvious that he had calmed from their time in the study, and was now wearing a patient, friendly look, suitable for dealing with the wayward child she felt like. 'I trust that I did not upset you too badly, just now.'

'No, Your Grace,' she said, resisting the urge to wipe away the beginnings of a tear. 'I am sorry. There was no reason for me to be in that room, and even less for looking at the ledgers.'

'I saw the rose, and thank you for it,' he said with another gentle smile as he came and sat beside her on the bed. 'It was a very nice gesture on your part, and as for the rest...'

'It will not happen again,' she said quickly. Of course, that meant that the books would remain wrong. And the thought of that five pounds and fifty pennies she had found, carrying from page to page, itched like horsehair next to the skin. Or perhaps it was just the nearness of him that was affecting her. She was strangely aware of him, as if they were touching, though several inches of space separated their bodies.

'I'd have found the problem eventually,' he assured her, seemingly unaware of the tumult he was creating in her soul. 'Or my man of business would have. The task of righting the books normally falls to him.'

'Of course,' she said, feeling foolish. Her husband was a great man, with many servants and employees scattered in multiple houses. He had no need of her help on a thing like this, since it was something normally left to someone else.

'He does not even want me playing with them, if I am honest,' Evan said with a wry smile. 'But it is my job to oversee all the workings of the estate. So, he must bear with my attempts.' Now, he cast his eyes down modestly, as if to say the mistakes were, of course, few and far between.

'I will not meddle again,' she promised, trying

not to feel disappointed. 'But I will admit, such things do fascinate me. Maths of all kinds...'

'How frustrating for you,' he said, tipping his head to the side to look directly into her eyes. 'I mean, that is not normally a subject that ladies have much use for.'

It was true. But, as it always did, the truth rankled. She smiled at him again and shrugged. 'The fact that it is not useful does not matter for men, does it? I am sure that you studied many things in school that you have not had much use for. Greek, for instance. You read it, don't you?'

'Of course,' he said.

'And are many documents you find on a day-to-day basis written in Greek?'

He paused, silent and surprised, then said, 'It helps us understand history.'

'And mathematics. They taught you more than you needed to manage in parliament, didn't they?'

'To focus the mind. To teach patience.' He looked less sure of himself now but went on. 'It helps to have a well-rounded education, I am told.'

'So, you admit that you have learned things that you had no real use for, just because everyone else learned them.'

He nodded. 'I suppose I have.'

'Then, is it really so unusual that I would learn things I did not need, just for the pleasure of it?'

'Pleasure,' he said, savouring the word as if he was thinking of things quite different than account books. 'I suppose there is no harm in seeking pleasure in something like learning. There are much riskier forms of hedonism than that,' he finished with a grin.

She nodded, though she had no idea what he might be talking about.

'As long as it does not detract from your other duties,' he added.

Her other duties. She did her best not to laugh at the idea that the trivial tasks he had mentioned to her that morning were the sort of things that could be interfered with. What was one less pressed flower in the world, after all? 'It will not,' she assured him with a smile. 'And I will not bother with the ledgers again. I will make sure that my studies are purely theoretical and will not let them distract me from anything important.'

'Very good,' he said, his smile returning to its original brilliance. And then he laid his hand on hers in a gesture of reassurance.

The simple touch resonated in her, like a bell ringing in her soul. She stared down at their hands, together but not quite joined, wishing she had the nerve to turn hers and link their fingers.

As if sensing her desire, he reached out with his other hand, clasping hers. The warmth of them flooded through her and she leaned into him, craving more.

'I am not like your father,' he said in a voice as soft as his touch. 'I may be cross at times. But I will never hurt you.'

'I know,' she replied, afraid to meet his eyes lest he see she was lying. She did not know. But right now, as they sat so close together that their shoulders were touching, she wanted to believe that her life could be different.

He withdrew from her slowly, as if he'd enjoyed the moment as much as she had. 'I will see you at dinner.'

'Until later, then,' she whispered, wondering what would happen between them in the many nights ahead.

That night's dinner was comparatively uneventful. They sat at the table, making polite conversation as if the incident in the study had never happened, and retired to the sitting room after. And once again Maddie wondered what it was that she was expected to do with her time. The meal was easier, with silverware to occupy her hands and the excuse of a full mouth to hide any lulls in conversation. But the silence in this room was oppressive, and she could not help the feeling of being on display, like a piece in a museum observed by an audience of one.

The feeling intensified as they took their seats on opposite sides of the fire. She had not taken the time to search the library for a book, nor could she think of a thing about their day apart that had not already been discussed over dinner.

In desperation, she called for a footman to bring her a mending basket, but even that was near to empty, holding a single torn shirt. Probably because she had informed the housekeeper that she did not want to be bothered with mending and was happy to turn it over to one of the maids. Now, she realised her mistake for there was nothing left but a small pile of linen squares ready to be hemmed into handkerchiefs. If she meant to entertain her husband with her non-mathematical skills for the whole of an evening, she would have to stitch very slowly.

She could not imagine a more pointless way to spend an evening, but she adjusted her chair so the light from the fire could shine on her lap and set to work.

On the other side of the room, the Duke took up a book, then looked up at her. 'Would you like me to read aloud?'

'That would be nice,' she said, relieved that they were not to spend the evening in silence.

To her surprise, he chose a novel and not a sermon or some other dry subject, as her father would have. Then he began to read. He proved a most diverting narrator, changing his voice with each new character and reading with expression and enthusiasm. It gave her one more way to admire him. His voice was pleasant and easy to listen to, and the story made her laugh. It was good that she had the sewing to tend to or she'd have found herself staring at him, and hanging on his every word.

As the hour grew late, and the stack of finished work grew, she wondered how many handkerchiefs a household could possibly need. She must find a way to make the task take longer or she would run through it on the first night. Rummaging through the basket, she found a skein of fine white silk and she threaded a fresh needle and began the painstaking process of embroidering a monogram in the corner of the first square.

She bit her lip, trying to decide how it should look. To do it properly, she should take the time to study the family crest and do that as well. Or perhaps she could try the motto. If she made a mistake tonight, she could always pick it out and start again tomorrow.

The needle slipped in her hand and pricked her finger. She stared down at the drop of blood forming, then quickly set her work aside and fumbled in her sleeve for her own unembroidered handkerchief to wipe away the red.

Her husband paused in his reading and asked, 'What are you making?'

The bleeding staunched, she held up the handkerchief she had been working on. 'It is barely started, of course. And it will need to be pressed.'

'Of course,' he agreed, taking it from her and examining it. 'But it is a fine thing all the same.'

He was lying. Her embroidery was a sad effort; the initials were small and crooked. But it was the best she could manage without time and a good pattern. Still, it was kind of him to ignore the fact. 'Thank you.' Then she added, 'I will try again tomorrow.'

He gave her a brilliant smile in response, and she felt herself blush. 'It pleases me that you are making such an effort to enter into the spirit of our marriage.'

'Thank you,' she said again, surprised that her bad embroidery could make up for any part of refusing his touch on their wedding night.

'My father spent much time teaching me the skills needed to be a good and loyal peer, but his instructions on choosing a wife were less rigorous.' He gave her a speculative look. 'I was to find a girl who was well-born, polite, obedient and accomplished, who would be an asset to me in social circles. And you are all of those things.'

She gave a nervous smile in return and doubted that accounting was anywhere on the list of accomplishments that the old Duke had been thinking of. Nor did she think she qualified as a social asset. In her only foray into London society, she had caused a life-changing scandal that had entrapped them both. But it was not as if she dared to contradict him on the subject. So she said, 'Thank you,' yet again. Then she changed the subject.

'But you say that your father had rules and standards for you as well?' Having a domineering father was at least something she could understand.

'Oh, yes,' he said with a wry laugh. 'I have spent my life trying to live up to the example he set for me.'

'What did he wish for you?' she said, honestly curious.

'First, I was to remember that once I took the coronet, I would no longer be my own man. Everything in my life would be done to give honour to the title. I must be honest and forthright in my dealings and demand similar standards from my family. Character was everything and reputation, once lost, could never be regained.'

'How very sensible,' she said, trying to ignore the nervous flutter in her stomach at the mention of family standards.

'I would be obligated to care for the estate. Not just the land, but the people. Their needs would come before my own.'

It was rather like having to sacrifice oneself for family. And this she understood perfectly. 'Go on.'

'I was to choose trustworthy staff and loyal friends. I was to pay the staff well and reward loyalty with loyalty.'

'And what happens to those who disappoint you?' she said cautiously.

'Very few have,' he said, with another smile to put her fears to rest. 'Many of the servants worked here when my father was alive. And as for friends?

I have Alex, who is as much a brother to me as if we had truly shared a mother.'

She could not help smiling back. 'And then he became a duke as well. I am sure your father would have been proud to hear that.'

'None of us expected that to happen,' Evan said quickly, and his expression faltered.

'All the same, I am sure Glenmoor benefitted from your father's wisdom and good example.'

The Duke shook his head. 'You have discovered the one flaw in my father's view of the world. He had little patience for people who had nothing to offer him. And a small boy who was not his heir held no interest for him.'

'How sad,' she said, shocked.

'You would not know it to talk to him,' the Duke replied. 'He shows no signs that my father's obvious favouritism for me bothered him. No bitterness towards life or towards me. And I have done my best to make it up to him, now that we are grown.'

'That is good, I suppose,' she said. But she could not help but feel sorry for the other man. 'And did your father have any other instructions for you?'

'Only that the continuation of the line was an important part of my duties,' he said.

There was a moment of awkward silence between them.

Then he hurried on. 'And the first step for that is to find a wife. Which I have done.' He was giving her a satisfied look, as if he had checked off a line on an imaginary list.

'I doubt your father would have approved of our meeting,' she said with a worried frown. 'It was hardly what anyone would call conventional.'

He gave a curious look. 'He was surprisingly reticent on the topic of courtship. It was not as if he expected me to dance attendance at Almack's and spend my days mooning over the latest crop of debutantes. He would have hoped for a favourable arrangement, much like the one your father made with Alex's cousin.'

'Oh.' He made marriage sound like nothing more than a financial transaction. It should not have surprised her, since that had been all she'd ever expected to have.

'You had land, after all,' he said, confirming her fears. 'And a sizeable dowry.' Then he brightened and added, 'And we married to preserve the family honour. He would have approved of that. It is the best reason of all to make an alliance. I am sure he would have had no patience at all with me if I'd married for love.'

'How fortunate that we did not do that,' she said.

Her sarcasm was lost on him for he nodded in agreement. 'He had no time for such foolishness. He often told me that since I would have my pick of eligible girls, the biggest challenge would be deciding which one would be the most helpful to the Dukedom.'

'I see,' she said, trying not to let the disappointment show in her face. She might have land and money, but there was nothing about her person or character that might distinguish her from the other girls making their come out this season. If it hadn't been for an outrageous accident, he would not have looked twice at her.

'But that does not mean that we will not suit well together,' he said hurriedly. 'Now that you know what is expected of you, I have every confidence in your ability to be a proper helpmeet.' He looked down at the handkerchief in his hand.

He probably thought that was a compliment, but it was nothing more than a thinly disguised sop to make her feel like she belonged here, when she clearly did not. She held out her hand for the linen, which was in no way fit for a duke. 'Give me that back. It is not done yet.'

Then his demeanour changed and his smile turned playful. 'Certainly not,' he said, holding the linen just out of reach. 'It is as fine a wedding gift as any man has received and I will carry it with pride.'

'I can do better,' she insisted, standing and stretching to reach it. He stood too.

'Oh, no, you don't. You have a basket of handkerchiefs by your chair. But this one is mine. It has my initials on it.' He tucked it into his pocket before she could snatch it back, and laughed as he grabbed her hands, holding them over her head to prevent her from trying again.

The move brought her body against his with a bump that left her too shocked to speak. Slowly, she raised her head to look up into his face, aware of the feel of him, hard against her, the smell of his cologne and the sight of his lips, inches from hers.

He must have felt something as well for his blue eyes turned dark as he stared down at her. 'You have given me a gift,' he repeated in a voice that seemed to envelop her like warm velvet. 'Now, what can I give you in return?'

Suddenly, it did not matter that he would not have

chosen her. He had married her. They were together here now, and she knew what she wanted.

She closed her eyes in invitation.

Then his lips came down to meet hers.

This was not like the brief peck on her wedding day. It was her first real kiss, and she wanted to remember it always. It was as warm and welcoming as one of his smiles, gentle and tender, undeniably sweet.

And then it was over and he released her hands, stroking down her arms until she dropped them to her sides, only to hold them again, his fingers twined with hers as if he did not want to let them go. 'We may have married for the most practical of reasons. But that does not mean that we won't be very happy together.' To prove the truth of this, he kissed her again.

When he released her, she swayed against him, resting her head against the lapel of his coat and rubbing her cheek against the wool, trying to memorise the comforting feel of it against her skin.

'You are tired,' he said, mistaking her behaviour as fatigue. He pushed her gently back onto her feet, and linked an arm with her, leading her out of the room and up towards their bedrooms.

She wanted to argue that she was not tired at all.

She had never felt more awake and doubted that she would be able to sleep at all. When they arrived in her doorway, he stopped to kiss her one more time, on the forehead. 'Goodnight, my dear. And do not worry. I think my father would be as pleased as I am.'

Chapter Six

The next morning Evan savoured his coffee over breakfast as Ramsey, who occupied the chair beside him, droned on about the latest stack of statements from the bank.

'Can this not wait until the meal is over?' he said, hoping that he did not sound as overwhelmed as he felt.

'I suppose it could,' the man said in a tone that implied it could not wait a moment longer. 'Or I could simply settle the matter myself and sign for you. There is the recent cheque from your brother, which has done much to improve the totals. But, as you can see from the lines here and here, it will be necessary to move the funds...'

Evan's mind wandered as the man pointed to something on one of the pages that might as well have been written in a foreign language. He stole a glance at the door, hoping that Madeline would come down to interrupt.

She had been so sweet the previous evening, working over her needlework as he'd read to her. When he had bothered to imagine a wife at all, he had hoped for someone just like that. It had been a white lie to say that his father would have approved of her. Evan doubted that the old Duke would have noticed her at all, other than to ask if she was increasing.

But then, his father had married a woman not prone to staying at home with her stitching. His stepmother had had a mind and money of her own and once the novelty of marriage to a duke had worn off, she had been with him as little as possible. Since it did not limit his access to her money, he was not bothered by her absence. The two of them had seemed to manage best when a distance of at least a hundred miles was kept between them.

But now his own sweet wife was there in the doorway, ready for her breakfast, and though he did not know her well, he doubted that such an arrangement would ever be needed.

He and Ramsey rose to greet her.

She looked from one to the other of them in surprise, then took her place and said softly, 'I did not realise we had a guest.'

'We do not,' Evan assured her with a smile, and took his seat again. 'This is John Ramsey, my man of business. You will see him often, now that he is back in London. He is my right hand in all things having to do with the management of my property.'

'Your Grace,' the man said with a deep bow to the Duchess.

'Mr Ramsey,' she said with a shy smile, and indicated that he be seated.

'I was just explaining to His Grace the need for certain transfers of funds in his investments.'

She glanced at the papers in front of him with obvious interest. 'Will you be taking care of the money in my trust as well?'

'That would be most efficient,' he said.

'But hardly necessary,' Evan corrected, pushing the papers aside. His father had married for money, and he had no intention of letting people think he had done the same. 'Your usual bankers will continue to handle the trust for you.'

'That will be fine as well,' she said with an amiable nod.

He nodded back at her and turned to Ramsey.

'I am sure it will not be necessary to access those funds.'

'Of course not, Your Grace.' Was there a trace of doubt on Ramsey's face when he said it? Even so, now was not the time to discuss matters which, with luck, could be put off indefinitely.

'And what are your plans for the day, my dear?' he said, turning back to his wife. 'Going shopping?'

'I suppose this is as fine a day as any to buy the new gowns you suggested,' she said.

'Very good.' It would make him feel somewhat less guilty about the money he had gained from the sale of her father's land if some portion of it was spent on her. 'And the guest list for a dinner?'

'I will ask Mrs Miller about it, right after breakfast,' she said.

'Excellent.' It would be the first step towards introducing his new wife to society and assuring the *ton* that there was nothing havey-cavey about their sudden marriage. He gave her another reassuring smile. Then he pushed the paperwork aside and turned to Ramsey before he could make any more comments about the need to draw funds from the principal. 'Let us take our coffee in the study and discuss this where it does not disturb my wife.'

The last thing he needed was to rekindle her interest in the finances, with Ramsey present. The man would laugh himself sick at the knowledge that Evan needed his wife to help him with his accounting.

After the men left the table Maddie stared pensively into her breakfast, wondering what her father would make of her husband's plan. It would probably anger him to think that she was to maintain control of her own money. He had intended it to be just one more part of the dowry to the Duke who would marry her.

Apparently, her husband felt differently. He had given her her money back and seemed enthusiastic that she spend it.

She had hoped that he had forgotten the suggestion that she buy a new wardrobe for she quite liked the one she already had. This morning she was wearing a new gown, and her maid had assured her that she looked her best. But the Duke had not even noticed it. He had just encouraged her to buy more clothing.

But he had also wished her to entertain, and she would send out invitations for the dinner party this morning. If she did not look the part, she was relieved that her handwriting was at least worthy of a duchess, clear, readable and elegant. She'd had multiple raps on the knuckles as a girl, until she had perfected the characters to her father's satisfaction and could write as well as anyone in her family. Her handwritten notes to his friends would be as fine as anything she could get from an engraver.

Once that was done, she would go to Bond Street. She sighed. She was still unsure just what it was that her husband meant by suitable clothing for a duchess. When she pictured duchesses, they were often much older and more dignified than she was. Perhaps he expected her to look more like her mother. Or perhaps it was his mother. With no portraits of either of the two previous duchesses in the townhouse, it was impossible to know what standard had been set.

Despite what he claimed, she wondered if Fallon regretted the choice of wife that had been forced upon him. She wanted to do her best to be the woman he did want, especially if it meant that there would be more moments like last night, when he had smiled and kissed her. For that brief span of time, she had felt that he might be growing to have real feelings for her, and not the polite kindness that seemed to be the hallmark of their marriage.

But perhaps kindness was more than she de-

served. The last few days had been both frightening
and happy. There had been no shouting or slapping.
Her husband did not just allow her to speak, he encouraged it and listened when she had something
to say. But she could not help thinking that, once
he truly knew her, it would all go back to the way
it had been before they had married.

But not today. Today, she would do everything he
had asked of her, and make him proud. When the
last of the invitations was stacked with the outgo-
ing mail, she called for the carriage and set out to
find a London dressmaker.

When she arrived on Bond Street, she scanned
down the row of shops in confusion. The best way
to find a good modiste was to take the recommen-
dation of friends. She would have none of those
until she had gone out in public with her husband
and received introductions. But she could not do
that until she had the appropriate clothes to wear.

It was all very puzzling.

With no one to guide her, she stepped into the
first shop she saw and hoped for the best. As she
entered, customers and shopgirls alike looked up,
took note of her clothes and manner and went back
to what they were doing without another glance.

She stood her ground for only a moment before

losing her nerve and backing out of the shop in embarrassment. It seemed her husband was right. She did not look like a duchess. Nor did she act like one, for she was sure a real duchess would know how to call attention to herself, just by walking into a room.

Since she had never seen a duchess before becoming one, she did not know what to do. Of the two dukes she had met, her husband, at least, had the presence to draw all eyes and command a room without uttering a word. But he had been trained from birth to be the man he was. How could she ask him to teach her something that had taken him a lifetime to learn?

And what help could he be to her right now, when she was standing alone on the pavement like a ninny, afraid to go forward or back? She glanced down the street at her carriage, with the distinctive crest on the door and the liveried grooms hanging from the back, ready to carry the packages she was supposed to be acquiring. With their green and gold uniforms, the grooms were far more impressive than she was in her modest country gown.

She waved down the coachman, who rolled the coach slowly up the street to her, and gestured to the grooms to come down from the coach, then pointed to the nearest modiste's shop. 'Open that door and hold it while I enter.'

Then she squared her shoulders and walked through the opening between the two burly men, into the shop.

She was pleased to see that this time the action inside stayed frozen as the shopkeeper left the magazine she had been reading and hurried up to her, then dropped into a curtsy. 'What may I help you with today, my lady?'

'Your Grace,' Maddie corrected quietly.

There was an audible gasp from the customers closest, then subdued whispering as they tried to guess whose wife she might be.

'I am recently married and need new gowns.' She gestured down at what she was wearing. 'Apparently, mine are unsuitable. But I do not know where to begin.'

The woman beamed. 'I can certainly help you with that, Your Grace.' As she led Maddie to a private fitting room, she clapped her hands once and a pair of shopgirls rushed to assist her, bringing sketchbooks and fashion plates and bolts of the finest cottons, wools and silks, in dazzling whites and rich colours. Then came the ribbons, the trims, the laces with embroidered hems, a profusion of fabrics greater than she'd ever been met with before. All were spread before her with playful flourishes, as if tempting her to touch each combination, and imagine them moving against her body as she danced.

Normally she did not enjoy shopping. It had always seemed a grim affair, where she was forced to stand stiff and still as a dress dummy while her mother and the modiste took turns hanging garments on her and commenting unfavourably about the way they fitted.

But things were different for a duchess. This dressmaker kept her supplied with tea and biscuits as she drew up an order for a vast array of evening gowns and day gowns that she assured Maddie would be necessary to carry any woman of fashion through the current season.

Maddie looked at the list, amazed. There were still some gowns from her last fitting that she had not worn, and a few garments that she was rather fond of. Perhaps she might keep those for days when she was not making or receiving calls. They had not been seen by anyone in London. She had only been here a week. And though she was sure that these new gowns would flatter her, they were not really to her taste. They were only what her husband wished for her to wear.

She wished to please him. But she should be able to please herself as well. There should be something that gave her comfort when she was not playing at being a duchess. She felt quite disobedient for crossing out a few of the items on the modiste's list, especially the new shifts and nightgowns. She had made a trousseau of those for herself before coming to London, stitching long hours into the night to get the tucks straight and the seams fine, with each completed garment approved by her mother, who had forced her to redo anything deemed too crooked or poorly made.

It had been a torturous project from start to finish. But after all the work she had put into the things, she meant to wear them to rags. It was not as if anyone would see them, after all.

Then she remembered that her husband was likely to see her underthings, and she blushed.

At this, the modiste proclaimed her overtaxed. She exchanged the tea for lemonade and assigned a shopgirl to fan her gently as the final arrangements for the bill were made. Who was her husband and to which bank should they send the account?

'The Duke of Fallon,' she said proudly.

The woman froze again, and for a moment the smile slipped from her face. 'Fallon.'

'Is there a problem?' she asked, surprised.

'No,' the woman said, in a way that clearly meant yes.

It was a matter of money. It had to be. What other reason would make a tradesperson flinch at the patronage of a duke? She had seen the totals in the ledgers, and the fact that the outlay for the season seemed to outstrip the income. Perhaps this wardrobe was an expense that her generous husband could not afford?

What was she to do to save embarrassment? The obvious conclusion occurred to her. 'The reckoning will go to my bank, since I have money of my own.' Why else would he have given her permission to manage her own money, if he did not intend her to pay her own bills?

She must have guessed the problem correctly for the modiste's demeanour changed and she answered with a relieved smile. 'It is a pleasure doing business with you, Your Grace.'

When she arrived home, it was with an order for a dozen new gowns. Hopefully, this was enough. But if she had to, she would go back and purchase more to satisfy the Duke.

She peered into the wardrobe at the dresses she

had brought from Norfolk before she had met him, wondering what was to be done with them. She ran her hands along her favourite, a white muslin with a deep embroidered hem that she'd had no reason to wear. Perhaps, after a few months of marriage, her husband would forget what he had thought was wrong with them and she could mix them in with her new gowns.

Then she closed the wardrobe door again and instructed her maid to pack most of them away. If she did not see them, it would be easier to put them from her mind. It was not such a great loss, after all, to be forced to wear things that were prettier and more expensive than she usually wore.

Her mother would think her a goose for worrying about it. Then she would remind Maddie that the true source of joy for a woman was a happy husband. She must learn to put her own desires last.

But that did not mean that she needed to set them aside completely. She had accomplished the tasks her husband had set for her, and there was still some time left in the day. Perhaps she could spend it as she wanted. Certainly not in accounting, for that had been a mistake she would not make again. But there was no reason she could not indulge in her mathematical interests in some other way.

She doubted that she could explain to her husband the hunger that she felt when presented with an unsolved proof, or an unfinished equation. Of course, he did not seem to be the sort of man who took pleasure in working calculations in his spare time.

She might be wrong. Perhaps it was only the ledgers that he did not like. But as long as she did not invade his study, and stuck to more feminine pursuits in the evenings, there should be no problem in spending part of her days in mathematical contemplation. In that vein, she went off to search the house to see if there were any books in it that might be of interest.

Compared to the garden, the library seemed dark and secretive. There was something about being here that felt as forbidden as the study. Perhaps it was the furniture, which was heavy and masculine compared to the delicately turned wood in her bedroom. Instead of lavender, the air had a faint smell of tobacco, even though she had never seen her husband smoke. Maybe the previous Duke had left his mark here, just as he'd left an imprint on his son.

She scanned the shelves, working her way through novels and history and poetry until she found a single book on calculus, which, unfortunately, was written in French. Cursing herself for not paying better attention in her modern language lessons, she pulled it down and riffled though the pages. Perhaps she did not need to know too much to understand it. She set it on the table and continued to look.

The shelves held nothing more of interest. But in a basket of old newspapers set aside as starters for the fire, she found a stack of outdated *Ladies' Diary* periodicals.

It was not as if she was the only woman with an interest in mathematics, and these were the proof. The *Ladies' Diary* magazine had a section with mathematical enigmas and word puzzles in it, and readers competed to discover the best answer.

When her father had caught her reading it, he had informed her that a woman's brain was not strong enough to withstand the stress of such things and had taken it away from her. He would rather see her reading *La Belle Assemblée*, which had lovely stories, but was too full of fashion plates for gowns she never wanted to wear. They made her feel foolish and useless, rather like the gowns she had bought today.

But there was no one stopping her from reading the *Diary* now. She leafed through the old magazines to find that the puzzle pages were all intact with no sign that they had been worked over, no scratches in the margins or scribbles along the binding. Who had bought them? she wondered. She had heard that gentlemen sometimes enjoyed working the problems, which were quite challenging. She doubted that her husband harboured a secret penchant for maths.

It did not matter who had left them. They were hers now. She clutched the magazines to her breast in glee, then set them carefully aside with the calculus. Then she considered. Where else in the house would one store mathematics texts? The nursery schoolroom, perhaps?

She crept up the stairs feeling quite subversive as she let herself into the nursery wing and searched the shelves. There were a few books that she had already studied, and one on trigonometry that she had not seen at all. Beside it were the copybooks that the students had used to meticulously copy out the statements from their schoolbook, to aid in memorisation.

The one for Master Alex was a tidy thing with neat rows of equations in a fine hand for a young man. Devoid of blots and ink-stains, it was so clear that she might as easily have learned from it as the textbook.

The book for Master Evan was another matter entirely. The lines of text were uneven, full of mistakes and cross-outs, as if, even when presented with the exact matter he was meant to commit, he could not seem to record it, much less understand.

All the same, the boy who would one day become Duke of Fallon had plugged away at it until the end of the book, showing no sign of aptitude even unto the last page.

She closed the book again, puzzled. How could a man who could not manage his schoolroom maths manage to keep the estate books in order? She had seen his work yesterday, full of blots and mistakes, just as this copybook was.

He had said that Mr Ramsey kept track of everything for him. What other choice would he have but to do as his father had instructed him and trust his employees to take care of the things he could not?

She replaced the copybooks and took the trigonometry book to her room, then went back to the library to get the book and magazines that she'd found to hide them in her room as well. Perhaps hide was the wrong word, but there was something about the collecting of these books that felt more secretive than it should have. She was sure, for the moment, at least, that she did not want to share the joy of her little cache with anyone.

She did not want to be warned against kindling a fever in her brain or upsetting her delicate female nerves. She did not want to stop learning, not for anyone. And sometimes it was easier to get forgiveness than to ask permission, especially from a husband who had his own demons when it came to calculation and seemed to have very specific views of what was and was not proper in a wife.

Chapter Seven

Evan was enjoying a whisky at White's, waiting for dinner, when Alex dropped into the chair beside him and signalled the waiter for a drink of his own. 'How goes it, brother?'

'Well,' Evan said with a satisfied smile. He had not enjoyed the primary privilege of marriage, as of yet. But that was all the more reason to smile, since the lack was not something he wanted to reveal to his brother or the world.

'Marriage suits you,' Alex said, giving him an assessing look.

'It does.' He agreed hesitantly, for it was hard to pinpoint a change in his habits, other than that he had company at meals. But he supposed there was a feeling of completeness about his life that he had not noticed before taking in Madeline. This must be what his brother sensed in him. 'Things are much as they were, but better,' he added. 'She adds a grace to the old house that was not there before.'

'Not when my mother was mistress of the house, at least,' Alex added with a roll of his eyes and a lift of his glass, to toast his lost mother. 'She'd have been appalled to be described thus. You talk of your wife as if you had purchased new draperies for the rooms.'

'That is not what I mean at all,' he said, trying to find a way to explain what he felt after three days of marriage. 'Madeline is quite different from your mother,' he managed at last. 'Quiet. One might even say timid. Very cooperative. It is as if she desires to make no ripple in her surroundings.'

'Good,' Alex said, taking another sip of his liquor. 'Because after today's rumours, I had feared...'

'Rumours?' Evan said, surprised.

'Apparently she took Bond Street by storm, marching into Madame Annette's Modiste accompanied by liveried servants. Then she spent a small fortune.'

'I may have had something to do with that,' Evan said with an embarrassed smile. 'Not the livery, of course. I would never...' Such ostentation should not be necessary. Though it was the sort of thing that his stepmother might have done, when she was alive.

'She had the servants hold the door, placed an extravagant order and then she announced that you should not be bothered and that she would be paying her own bills,' Alex added.

'She most certainly will not,' Evan said firmly. 'I am quite capable of covering the cost of a few gowns.'

'Of course you are,' Alex said. 'I am only mentioning it because you describe her as shy. And when she is not with you, her behaviour seems nothing of the kind. And her father...'

'She is nothing like her father,' he said, horrified at the thought.

'And apparently nothing like my mother, other than her shopping and her wealth,' Alex completed for him with a shake of his head. 'But I must know, would it truly be so bad if she were to pay her own bills? It might teach her a sense of economy to manage her own finances.'

Evan winced at the thought. It reminded him of the way she had been poring over the account books. 'If anything, she has too much sense already.

I would not want people to think that I had married her for the money.'

'Hmm,' said Alex, taking a sip of his whisky.

'And what does that mean?' he snapped.

'Well, that was not the only thing on your mind when you offered for her. But wasn't that why you encouraged me to marry her? You could not stop talking of the land I would gain. You said marriage was a transaction.'

'That was different,' he said.

'In what way?'

It was different because Alex did not think that he was failing at the one thing he had been trained to do. Despite the sudden change in his status, he had adjusted to it well and had no trouble managing his estate and his finances. He was not in continual debt and trouble, as Evan seemed to be.

He took another drink and said curtly, 'Because that was you and this is me.'

Alex held up an apologetic hand as if recognising that he had overstepped the bounds of the closest of friendships. 'I will say no more. Another drink, I think, and then do you fancy a game of billiards?'

Evan nodded, gritting his teeth. A game of billiards and then he would go home and have a talk with his wife.

* * *

It had been a satisfying afternoon, sitting in the library and working one of the puzzles found in the old magazines, a tricky question that involved estimating the height of a bird in a distant tree, while accounting for the curvature of the earth. When she heard her husband come in the front door, she put aside her work and went out to the hallway to greet him.

But he strode past her, uttering a single word. 'Madeline.'

She flinched. Nothing good had ever come of being addressed by her full name in that tone. Now he stopped in the doorway of his study and turned back to her. 'Come here.' Though his voice was gentle, there was something in his stature that proved he was angry with her.

She walked towards him, trying not to drag her feet. Then she followed him into the room and watched as he closed the door behind them. Perhaps this, whatever it was, would be the thing that would finally drive him into a rage. She did not like to have anger directed towards her, but after years of dealing with her father, three days of relative civility had been surprisingly hard on the nerves.

He went to his place behind the desk and indicated a chair, which she took. Then he said with a deceptively calm smile, 'What did you do today?'

'I went to Bond Street,' she said, and could not help adding the rebellious thought, *as you requested.* 'To the modiste. And a milliner. And a shoemaker.' Now that she said it, it sounded as if she had been spending too freely, despite the fact that he had wanted her to shop.

'Accompanied by servants?' he said with a raised eyebrow.

'I did not know how else to get the attention of the shopkeeper,' she said, feeling rather foolish now that she was questioned about it.

He sighed. 'I suppose it was necessary, since few people in town know you. But in the future such a show of wealth will not be necessary. My father always said you must learn to enter a room with a confidence that will show others you deserve their respect.'

'Oh,' she said, feeling not the least bit confident. His father might have taught him to command respect, but hers had spent nearly as many years teaching her to be quiet and draw no attention to herself.

Apparently, he assumed the matter was settled,

for he went on. 'And when it came time to settle the bills, did you have them sent to my bank, or to Ramsey?'

For a moment she was afraid to say anything at all. It was clear, by the sound of the question, that he already knew the answer, and that he was not happy with it. How he could have found out so soon was a mystery to her. But if he had, there was no point in lying. 'No,' she said, and could feel herself tremble as she waited for his response.

'Why not?'

'The modiste did not seem comfortable with the idea.'

'Really?' he said, still in a mild tone. 'And it matters to you, does it, whether shopkeepers are comfortable doing business with me?'

'I had funds of my own, which you said I could control. And a new wardrobe seemed like such a self-indulgent expense that I thought it would be better to spend my own money.' She said the words in a rush, as if that would make things easier for both of them.

'And do you understand that it does not speak well of our relationship if you do not trust me to pay my bills?'

'I trust you,' she insisted.

'The rumour is already about that I have married you for your money. Your taking on major expenses only reinforces that. And the best way for me to quell the gossip that I have a problem paying my bills is to receive some and settle them, as I was quite capable of doing.'

'I did not think,' she said. That was perfectly true. But it was also true that the rumours of him being in debt had existed before their marriage. Her father had mentioned the fact to her himself.

But apparently no one cared. No one except the shopkeepers whose bills would not be paid. And, though he might not like the answer, it did bother her that the woman had been upset. 'Would it be such a bad thing if you used my money?' she said softly. 'I do not mind.'

'But I do,' he said. 'Despite what people might think, I have the money to pay for your wardrobe.'

As she understood it, it had come from the Dukes exchanging the Goddard land between them. But it would not do to explain to him that, in a way, she was still paying for her own clothing, merely by a more circuitous route. She responded with a quiet, 'Oh.' Then added, 'I am sorry. It will not happen again. But you said I was to maintain control of my own money. If I am not to spend it, what am I to do with it?'

He did not speak for a moment, as if the question surprised him. Then he said, 'Invest it, I suppose. But I do not recommend you take my advice in the matter. It embarrasses me to admit it, but I do not have the natural talent that some men have for managing money. If I were to take on your fortune, it would be gone as quickly as mine was.' He looked away for a moment, ashamed to meet her eyes. 'It is better that you keep it aside. Because, if you do not yet trust me in all things, how can I take on the control of your money? Do you understand?'

He was right. She did not fully trust him. Not to pay the bills, not with her body and certainly not with her safety, if she was still half expecting him to strike her after each disagreement. 'I understand,' she said slowly.

Then his face brightened. 'Some things will change with time. We must both be patient. And we will not let a minor disagreement cast a cloud over our future.'

And, as always seemed to happen when he smiled at her, her doubts evaporated and she felt ridiculously happy and sure that things would be better, just as he promised. 'All right,' she said, 'it will be as you wish.'

* * *

But the next day she was sitting in the morning room when Mr Ramsey appeared in the doorway, announcing his arrival with a polite cough.

She looked up from the enigma she had been working and smiled. 'Mr Ramsey, is there something you require?' Her husband was out of the house, as he always was during the day. But his man of business seemed to come and go as he pleased, working at a table in the library, or gathering papers in the study without the presence of his master.

'If I might speak to you for a moment, Your Grace?'

'Of course,' she said, setting aside her work.

He paused and glanced behind him to make sure the hall was empty of servants, as if the matter was one of some delicacy and he did not want to be overheard. Then he murmured, 'It is about His Grace, and the accounts.'

What else would it be about? But after their most recent discussion on the matter of money, she suspected that the Duke would see having similar chats with Mr Ramsey as a betrayal of trust. She responded in the way she assumed her husband would want her to. 'I am not to have any business with those. My husband made that clear before you arrived.'

He nodded. 'I saw the strange hand in the account books. I wondered if it might be you.'

'I glanced at the ledgers and made some corrections,' she admitted. 'It was not my place to do so and will not happen again.'

'Do not worry. I have no intention of asking you to do anything that is forbidden. But I wondered if you might use your influence to sway his mind on certain subjects.'

Her influence. She resisted the urge to laugh at the suggestion that she might in some way be able to change the mind of a man who was so obviously in control of his world. Then she composed herself and asked, 'What do you mean?'

'It is the matter of the money that has been given to you as part of your dowry,' he said, pausing again as if he hesitated to suggest what was coming. 'I do not think the Duke is fully aware of the depth of his need, and the breadth of his expenses.'

That was quite possibly true. But he had also made it clear that it was none of her concern. Still, if his man of business was worried, perhaps she had reason to worry as well. 'And what do you want me to do about it?' she asked, suspecting that she knew the answer.

'If your money was combined with his, it would relieve certain pressures on the finances,' he said with an earnest smile.

'But he has already expressed his desire that my money remain separate,' she said.

'What are your opinions on the matter?' he asked gently.

She considered. She had opinions, of course. But being asked for them was a novelty. The only man in her life, until a few days ago, had had no desire to hear them expressed. And though her husband was more liberal, she had no idea how far his patience would stretch.

At last, she decided a white lie would be best. 'I have none of my own. For one thing, I lack the information needed to make a decision. And, for another, I do not want to go against my husband's wishes.'

'So, you disagree with him,' Mr Ramsey said, seizing on the thing she had hoped to hide in her statement. 'If it were totally up to you?'

'I would not object to combining our funds and allowing my husband to manage my money. I trust him,' she added, since that was the thing he had been most concerned about. But, even as she said it, there was a niggling doubt that it was the right thing to do. 'It is his to do with as he wishes. And he wishes the money to remain separate from his control,' she said in a firmer tone, to settle the matter in her mind.

'But you have no objections,' Ramsey said, once again listening only to the words he wanted to hear. 'Now, we just have to persuade him.'

'We?' she said doubtfully. 'I am sorry, but I do not think that is within my power to do.'

'Not yet, perhaps,' he said. 'But in time things may change, both for you and for him. When that happens, please consider what I am suggesting. It may mean the difference between solvency and insolvency for the whole estate.'

Surely things were not that bad. If they were, she should not have bought so many pointless gowns. Her extravagance could be the ruin of them. But would her husband realise that? And was it her place to tell him? He had told her specifically not to worry, and that he could afford the expense. But suppose he had lied to spare her feelings?

Her thoughts were racing, but she gave Mr Ramsey what she hoped was a reassuring smile. 'I can make no promises. But I will keep what you have said in mind. If I find a good time to broach the subject with my husband, I will do so.'

He smiled, relieved. 'That is all I can ask of you, Your Grace. Thank you for your time.' Then he turned and left her alone again.

Chapter Eight

The night of the dinner party arrived without further incident. As his valet tied his cravat, Evan marvelled at the smoothness of the preparations and the fact that there was no sign of the hustle and bustle that had taken place, above or below stairs.

For her part, his wife had been as quiet as she always was, showing no obvious nervousness at the prospect of entertaining a room full of dukes and duchesses that she had never met before. He heard no sounds from the room next to his, no slamming of doors or banging of drawers, and no raised voices or snapping at the maids.

This current peace was very different from when his stepmother had ruled the house. He and Alex had known to steer clear of her in the days before any gathering or party, when her already short temper was always frayed to nothing.

He glanced at the leather jewel box on his dresser and smiled. The necklace inside it had been a rare gift from his father to Alex's mother and the only piece of Fallon jewellery that was stored in London. It was also one of the few fond memories he had of that couple's marriage. He recalled how happy the lady of the house had been when she'd received those diamonds and how proud she'd been to wear them, on the rare times she and the Duke were seen together.

His valet gave his coat a final brush and declared him finished and Evan smiled at his reflection, well satisfied. After dismissing the servant, he took up the jewel case and strode to the connecting door. He reached for the handle, then drew back, not wanting to try it and find it still locked.

He did not yet feel entitled to come and go as he pleased from his wife's room. But he had spent the two weeks of their marriage working to break down her defences. Each evening before bed, he had walked her to her room and said his goodnights with a kiss, taking care that each one was a little bolder and longer than the last. He had not been so daring as to open her mouth, as yet. But last night, when he had brushed the side of her breast with his fingertips, she had not pulled away.

The results of these experiments had been favourable. She had begun to look expectantly at him when bedtime drew near, to smile as he took her in his arms and to leave him with sighs that were one part happiness and one part disappointment.

This prolonged seduction excited him in a way he had not experienced before. Self-denial was unfamiliar to him. Before this, his habit was to bed experienced women, the sort who responded favourably to the first suggestion of a quick tumble and held no expectations of more than that.

But with each day spent waiting for Madeline, he had grown to want her a little bit more. This morning at breakfast he had been so fascinated with the graceful curve where her neck met her shoulder, and the slight swell of her breasts each time she sighed that he'd been unable to answer when she had offered to pour his coffee.

She had ignored his silence and prepared the cup anyway, but she had done it with a little smile that made him wonder if she knew the cause of his distraction and felt something similar herself.

He took it as a sign that tonight's kiss would overcome the last of her resistance and he would cross the threshold of her room and find paradise.

But not before dinner. He rapped gently on the door. 'Madeline?'

'Come in,' she said from the other side, adding, 'it is unlocked.'

He grinned and opened the door.

She was staring at herself in her bedroom mirror with a dazed expression as if she could not quite believe the reflection cast back belonged to her. And she did look quite different from her usual, innocent self. He assumed she was wearing one of the new dinner gowns, a stiff blue satin pelisse with long ruched sleeves and a scalloped hem over a high-waisted silver gown. To match it, her hair had been piled high on her head and dressed with ostrich plumes that made her look far taller than her rather diminutive height.

She glanced at him in the mirror, then turned to face him, as if relieved to be turning away from her own image. 'I do not look like myself,' she said with a wry smile.

'But you are lovely, all the same,' he said, giving her an approving nod. 'And I have brought you something that will match the gown.' He walked to her dressing table, opened the case and held out the necklace to her.

'You shouldn't have,' she said, staring at the jewels in dismay. 'It's too much.'

He laughed. 'You did not think I would let you be the only woman at the party with a bare neck?'

'But the cost,' she said, still hesitant.

'It is an old family piece,' he replied, reaching out to her so he could fasten it around her neck. Then he turned her back to the mirror so she could see it. He left his hands on her shoulders, staring down at the soft white flesh of her throat, and imagined kissing where the jewels lay.

She reached out a hesitant finger and ran it along the gold setting. Then she reached up and covered his hands with hers. 'Thank you,' she whispered.

'You look beautiful, my dear,' he said.

'Do you really think so?'

He nodded. 'And I am amazed by my own luck in finding you.'

As he watched, she blinked her large green eyes slowly, and a flush crept from the pillows of her breasts up into her cheeks. Tonight would be the night. He was sure of it. But he must release her now, before temptation got the better of him and he forgot that a long, proper evening lay ahead for them.

As if she realised what he was thinking, her

hands dropped away from his and she offered him another shy smile. 'If you will excuse me, Your Grace, I must go check with Cook to see that everything is in order.'

'Of course,' he said. 'Until later then.'

After he was gone, Maddie hurried out of the room and down the stairs to the kitchen. As she had suspected, there was nothing that needed her attention. But after the visit from her husband she needed to do something to settle her nerves.

He approved of her.

She was relieved, of course, but could hardly believe it was true. She had looked at herself in the mirror, dressed in satin and feathers, and had hardly recognised herself. The addition of diamonds and a handsome man gazing at her with undisguised longing had done nothing to make it more believable.

Perhaps, later, she could fall back into that dream and allow it to carry her away. But now, what she needed was something to calm her, before the crowd arrived and she had to spend the rest of the night pretending to be in control and at ease. She clasped her trembling hands and turned to the cook and the housekeeper with a falsely confident smile. 'All seems to be in order and there is still some time before the guests begin arriving. If I am needed, I shall be in the library.' Then she ran.

Behind her, the mantel clock struck seven, shocking her back to reality.

She had been working for almost forty-five minutes, lost in the elegance of a sine wave that she had graphed into her notebook. The guests would not be arriving for at least another half an hour. The Duke had not yet come down from his bedroom. She could steal a few more minutes for herself.

She dipped her quill in the ink and carefully copied the equation from the text at her left into the journal in front of her, admiring the smooth flow of the variables, and committing it to memory as she wrote.

From behind her, someone tapped on the frame of the open door.

She turned. It was Glenmoor, who she should now think of as a brother and not as the man she had almost been forced to marry. She set the quill aside and smiled. 'Good evening, Your Grace.'

'I am early, I think,' he said. 'But I am used to coming and going from this house as if it is my own and forgot how rude it would seem to you.'

'Then there is no way for you to be too early, Your Grace,' she said, sanding the writing to set it.

'Please, call me Alex,' he said, his smile even brighter than it was before.

'Of course,' she said, 'since we are family now. And you must call me Maddie.'

'What are you doing there?' he said, coming close enough to look over her shoulder.

She resisted the urge to slam the book shut so that he could not see. But really, there was nothing very shocking about the task she'd set for herself, so she admitted the truth. 'Calming my nerves.'

'With a trigonometry copybook?' he said with a laugh.

'That is the point of copybooks,' she said. 'To study the subject by writing it out is an excellent way to commit things to memory and, frankly, I find it soothing.'

'Then you are most unlike your husband, who found such things a trial.'

'I saw,' she said. 'I visited the nursery and found his own copybooks from when he was a boy.'

Alex winced. 'You will find the later ones better than the first attempts. Eventually, he paid me to do the work for him. It was a rather nice supplement to my allowance.'

'He cheated,' she said, shocked.

'Only in small ways,' Alex assured her. 'He is not stupid. He can declaim in Greek and Latin and speak knowledgeably on a wide variety of subjects. He worked very hard to grow into the man that his father expected him to be. It is just mathematics that he cannot seem to comprehend.'

'That is unfortunate,' she said. She had suspected as much, but it was still disappointing to learn the truth. 'I like maths of all sorts.'

'I imagine you do, if you are studying trigonometry before dinner. Does Evan know of your hobby?'

'His Grace has been adamant that I may do as I like with my time,' she said, evading the question. 'And while I understand it is not to his taste, it is not necessary for husbands and wives to share interests,' she added, putting away her books and sliding into her gloves. 'In fact, it would be unusual for that to be the case.'

'That is because women tend to have interests that are of little use to gentlemen,' Alex said with a smile. 'Trimming bonnets and painting still lifes...'

'Why do you suppose it is that women are forced into such tedious pursuits?' she snapped back, surprising herself. Then she added in a milder tone, 'It is not as if we all enjoy them. But if we do not pretend to, we are deemed unmarriageable.'

'Well, I believe that there is nothing unmarriageable about a woman who prefers maths to arts and crafts. In fact, I would prefer such a woman, if I could find one.'

'Really?' Her husband was standing in the doorway of the room, leaning against the door-frame in a way that was intended to be casual, but looked anything but. 'I had no idea you had such strong opinions about marriage.'

'I hadn't given it much thought,' Alex said, giving him a bland look in response.

'If you leaned in such a direction, you had your chance,' Fallon said with a faintly menacing smile. 'You did not take it.'

'No, I did not,' Alex replied with a knowing smirk. 'But I will admit to being fascinated by the fact that you did. The two of you are an interesting pairing. And you cannot blame me for wanting to know my new sister a little better, can you?'

'If that is how you view her, no, I do not.'

Maddie looked from one man to the other, confused. It sounded almost as if her husband was jealous, which was ridiculous. He had no reason to be. But to break the tension in the room, she rose and stepped between them. 'In any case, it is almost half past seven. The other guests will be arriving soon, and I must speak to the butler and check on the wine.' She smiled at the pair of them and said, 'If you will excuse me, Alex?'

'Of course,' he said with a bow and a grin, then nudged his brother. 'Maddie calls me Alex now.'

She could not help a flush of pleasure at the sight of her husband's shocked expression, and the curious look he gave her as she passed him to check on dinner. Perhaps he was the one in need of a calming hobby.

A short time later the guests arrived and, after drinks and conversation in the salon, they processed to the dining room. Evan looked down the table at his wife, elegantly attired and presiding over the finest meal he'd had in a long time. With the help of the housekeeper, she had created a guest list made up of other peers and their wives and a dowager or two to balance the table. For his part, he was eager to introduce her to his equals, and to impress her with the powerful circle in which she now travelled.

It was a group that would have terrified the average woman and would have daunted even her gregarious father into silence. But she was managing well. She was quiet, of course. That could not be helped. The people around her were strangers to her and she was, by nature, shy. But she smiled often and listened more than she talked, and that never failed to impress the more senior members of the party, who liked to hear themselves speak.

During the dinner she displayed an easy mastery of the household, managing any small problems before they occurred. There was a moment at dessert where he quite feared that the ice was going to arrive early to the table, before the orange sponge that accompanied it, but she ordered the service of the footmen with barely perceptible signals of her hands, her smile never wavering.

She was like a swan on a pond. A ruffled blue satin swan, but a swan nonetheless. Graceful and serene. Despite earlier reservations, it seemed he had married the perfect woman.

After the meal the ladies retired, leaving the men to their port, and conversation as stuffy as the tobacco smoke filling the air.

The Duke of Manforth, a rather rotund older gentleman, leaned forward and nudged Evan in the ribs. 'I hear you swept your wife quite off her feet when you met her, eh, Fallon?' He chuckled at his own joke.

'We ran into each other in a garden,' Evan said with a tight smile. 'And were caught unchaperoned. It was a mistake, but a most fortuitous one on my part.'

'I can see that. Pretty, well-mannered and rich. An excellent combination in a wife.' Manforth reached for another glass of wine and drank deeply. 'And she was promised to Glenmoor originally, was she not?'

Evan had wondered how much of the story the *ton* knew, and apparently the answer was all of it.

This time, Alex answered for him. 'My loss, I'm sure. But the connection between them was instantaneous and, charming though Maddie is, I was not ready to marry.'

Maddie. There was that name again.

It was ridiculous to feel so sensitive about it. There was no reason to believe that Alex would do anything to spoil his marriage. The two of them were closer than most blood relations and had never wanted other than the best for each other.

But there was something about Madeline that reminded him of Alex. A quiet thoughtfulness before they spoke. Or perhaps it was the shared smiles he had seen in the library, or the way they leaned towards each other when they talked.

It was nothing really, and yet it rankled. And now that he was getting to know her, he could not shake the belief that Madeline deserved the better man. And despite how hard he'd worked to live up to his father's ideals, he suspected that Alex was the better of the two of them.

The question remained, what was he to do about it? Nothing, at least for now. Until the matter of an heir was settled, he was not about to allow her to take up with another man, even if the two of them were perfectly suited for each other. She was his wife, in name, at least.

But Manforth saw none of his doubts and, beaming at him, said, 'So it was a love match?'

What choice did he have but to lie? 'Can you look at Maddie and doubt the fact?' Evan said, proud that he did not stumble on the unfamiliar name. But be damned, if Alex used it, then he was more than entitled to. 'One look into those eyes, and I knew.' He said the last with surprising conviction, since he could not remember what he had thought when he had first looked into her eyes. He only knew that when he saw her now he felt a possessiveness that had been absent from their first meetings, a strange uneasiness that was all the stronger when he wondered what she thought of him.

'Well, let us join the ladies, then,' the old man said with a grin. 'The sooner we do, the sooner this houseful of people will be out of your hair and the two of you can be alone.'

Evan smiled and finished his drink in a gulp. Being alone with his wife was precisely what he'd planned at the beginning of the evening and was just the thing to set his foolish doubts to rest. By morning, there would be no question as to whom she favoured, or who had the right to call her Maddie.

It was close to midnight when the last of the guests had gone and Maddie could retire to her bedroom to change out of the unfamiliar costume and into her nightgown.

The evening had gone well. The food had been excellent, the conversation lively, and when she'd compared herself to the other wives in the room, she had looked the part of a duchess with her new dinner gown and diamond necklace.

Her husband's dazzling smiles had been bestowed liberally on her both during and after the meal. He had even whispered, 'Well done,' and pulled her close for a brief kiss as they'd passed each other in the hall while seeing people to the door.

He was proud of her. This should not be so un-expected, she supposed. Wasn't that why she acted the way she did? She was always trying to gain his approval. But she had not expected anything more than the solemn nods she'd sometimes got at home when she had done something to please her father. She certainly did not think she'd hear ac-tual words of praise or receive a kiss on the ground floor, where anyone might have seen them.

She glanced at the unlocked door that connected their rooms. Perhaps, if he was happy with her, to-night would be the night when they would consum-mate their marriage. The thought was more exciting than frightening. Instead of an intrusion, it seemed like the natural end to a successful day. If he did not come to check on her, she had even invented a reason to go to him. Although she had let the maid take down her hair and change her into her night-dress, she had requested the necklace remain where it was, so she might ask for help undoing the clasp.

It was a transparent scheme, she was sure. But since she lacked the nerve to request what she wanted from him—more kisses, more touches, more of his company in any way she could get it— she would need to create a situation where those things happened without words on the subject being exchanged.

She looked in the dressing table mirror, touching the sparkling cascade of stones that still hung between her breasts. She should have expected such a gift. She had known that dukes had family jewellery, and she had known that she would some day be a duchess. All the same, she had never imagined herself wearing such a splendid thing.

He had placed it around her throat so gently and stared at her in the mirror with such intensity that her entire body had tingled. She closed her eyes for a moment, remembering the feel of his hands on her shoulders when he had put it on her and imagining what it would feel like when he removed it.

Then she opened her eyes and squinted into the mirror, puzzled. One stone was not glittering as brightly as the others. Perhaps it needed a gentle cleaning, for she wanted nothing to mar the perfection of the moment that she went to him. She reached behind her and undid the clasp with no help needed. Then she stretched the necklace out on the table before her, trying to spot the problem she had seen in the mirror. And there, a little to the left of centre, she found a stone that did not sit properly in its setting.

It was probably nothing more than a bent prong that could be fixed with a hairpin and a bit of fiddling. But when she picked at the diamond with her thumbnail to wiggle it back into place, it popped from its setting and skittered across the surface of the table.

Oh, dear. This was not what she had meant to do at all. She dragged it back towards the necklace, embarrassed at the damage she had caused to her gift. If she was not careful, she would mar the surface of the table as well, for if diamonds were even harder than glass they must certainly be harder than varnish.

But that did not seem to be the case in this instance. As she moved it, she was surprised to feel the stone crack under her thumb. Perhaps it was already broken and that had made it fall out of its setting.

She frowned and picked the shards up on the tip of her finger. Diamonds did not shatter. But glass did.

She set it down again and looked away, wondering what she was to do now. Nothing good would come of further investigation. But if one stone was paste, what of the others? She had to know.

She turned her hand mirror face up on the table

and gently scratched it with the largest of the stones in the necklace. If it was a diamond, then surely it would leave a mark. But when she looked, the glass remained clear.

He had given her a paste necklace.

She told herself that it did not really matter. Even if it was false, it was prettier than anything she had ever worn before.

But why had he done it? Did he think that she was a foolish country girl who would never notice the truth? It did not say much for what he thought of her, if that was the case. And if there was such trouble with money, as there obviously was, why did he bother sending her off to Bond Street? Was everything about their life together as big a pretence?

Most importantly, why did he make such a show of wanting her trust, only to lie to her over such a silly thing as this? Didn't he understand that she had loved him from the first moment she'd seen him, and that lies would only diminish that first sweet feeling, making it seem cheap and silly? If she could not trust the necklace, how could she trust anything about this marriage?

Suddenly, she heard the door open behind her and when she glanced in the mirror she saw the reflection of the Duke standing in the doorway between their rooms, smiling at her. 'Did you enjoy the party?'

Without thinking, she opened the drawer of the dressing table and swept the necklace and its broken stone into it, then shut the drawer and turned to face her husband. She smiled back, surprised to feel the expression forced. 'Yes,' she said, 'it was a very nice evening.' At least it had been until recently, when things had taken an unexpected turn.

She pushed that to the back of her mind and asked, 'Was it as you hoped it would be?'

'All I hoped and more,' he said, and now there was a distinct fondness in the way he looked at her. 'You look beautiful.' He glanced at her bare throat. 'And did you appreciate my gift?'

Now she was sure that he must realise that something was wrong. He would know that she knew. But if he did not wish to tell her the truth, then she must pretend that she did not know it. 'I liked it very much,' she said. 'It was very kind of you to think of me.'

'When I have time, I will send for the things that are in the strongroom at Fallon Court, and we will deck you out properly. You shall be the most splendid woman in London.'

'You do not need to bother,' she said, both embarrassed and confused by his generosity.

'Of course I do,' he said, giving her an odd look. 'If you are to be my duchess, you will wear the jewels that belong in the family.'

As she feared, it was just another tradition and not any specific desire to please her. He must act like a duke and she must look like a duchess. 'All right,' she said, locking her smile into place and willing herself to show no sign of worry.

There was a pause and he smiled at her again, then stepped over the threshold and came to her. 'Well, then. It is time for bed, is it not?'

She nodded, feeling nervous again for what might come next. She had been wrong to think she was ready for this. Even after two weeks, they were still strangers in so many ways.

He bent down to kiss her, as he had each night of their marriage. But tonight, when it should have been easy, she could not seem to relax and accept it. Her lips would not mesh with his. Her body felt stiff and unyielding where, just a night ago, she had melted into him, praying that the moment would never end.

He must have sensed the strangeness as well, for he broke the kiss and gave her a puzzled smile.

'You are tired, I think. It has been a busy night for both of us.' He stood there for a moment, looking as awkward as she felt. Then he recovered his poise and turned to go. 'Sleep well, my dear.'

'And you, Your Grace,' she said.

At her words, he froze in the doorway between the rooms, then turned back to her with his most brilliant smile. 'Please, call me Evan.'

She blinked. 'Evan.' And then the door closed and he was gone.

Chapter Nine

The next morning, Evan sipped his breakfast coffee and pretended to sort through the post while considering the woman who sat down the table from him.

Something was definitely wrong with Madeline.

Maddie, he reminded himself. He was making an effort to put her at ease and should call her by her nickname. Unless that was the behaviour that was making things worse. If so, he did not know what to do.

'Did you enjoy the dinner last night?' he said, as casually as possible.

'It was very enjoyable, Evan. Thank you for introducing me to your friends.'

Her answer sounded right, and she had used his first name as he'd requested. But he could not shake the feeling that there was something more that she was not saying.

But then, he had his own unspoken questions. Why had last night's wonderful evening not ended in her bed? When he had given her the necklace, he'd been convinced that he could have seduced her there and then had he tried. The unlocked door between them had been another sign of willingness. He'd gone to her room and found her pink, pliable and eager.

But before big events women hated to have their hair mussed and their dresses wrinkled, no matter how much fun it was. More importantly, there was only one chance to love her for the first time, and he was not about to rush the moment.

So he had waited until later. Apparently, that had been too late. A night's rest had not changed things. This morning she seemed friendly, but as distant as she had been in the early days of their marriage.

Had someone said something to her, he wondered, that had put her out of the mood? He was tempted to blame Alex again, but she'd shown no particular partiality to the fellow later in the evening. She'd wished him a cordial goodnight, but nothing more than that.

Perhaps it was only a passing mood, and he could win her over again with a night out. He raised the letter he was holding, waving it temptingly in the air. 'I trust the previous evening did not tire you too much.'

'Of course not,' she said, as agreeable as ever.

'Before we married, I committed to attending the Dowager Duchess of Wainstaff's ball this evening. She writes to assure me that you are included in the invitation and hopes to see us.'

She blushed prettily at the idea and said, 'I will respond with thanks, and assure her that we will be there.'

'Good,' he said, taking another sip of his coffee. 'I will call for the carriage at seven and we shall make our first public outing together.' And, hopefully, the night would be magical enough to pull his wife from her mood and lure her back into his arms.

Maddie kept her smile in place until her husband left the room. Once he was gone, she pressed her hands to her cheeks to wipe the expression away. Another social event, and so soon. She had hoped for some respite after last night's dinner, and some time to decide what to do about the necklace before she was called upon to wear it again.

She supposed that it was inevitable that they would be popular this season. The suddenness of their marriage had been a source of fascination to the guests on the previous evening, and she expected more questions on the subject tonight. If they were to have any peace, they would have to show the world that they had a perfectly happy union and were not holed up at home, hiding their incompatibility from the *ton*.

But were they normal? She really had no idea how properly married people behaved. She had only her parents as an example, and she'd have described them as more resigned than happy. But at least they were intimate, or so she assumed.

She thought longingly of the kisses that the Duke had given her thus far, reminding herself to think of him as Evan. Despite the matter of the necklace, he had been a very understanding husband to her. She must try to be a good wife to him. There would be no more awkwardness between them, and no more refusing of his advances. Then, when people wondered at the details of their marriage, she would not feel like such a liar when she proclaimed that they were happy.

That night she dressed with care in a rose silk satin with a deep décolletage and a skirt embroidered in gold flowers. As the dinner gown had, the ball gown felt odd to her, as if she was wearing someone else's clothing. It was very beautiful, but it was not her.

Fortunately, the false diamonds did not complement the neckline, so she did not have to explain the damage she had done to them. Instead, she chose the long string of pearls that had been a wedding gift from her parents. They lay against the satin, reflecting the pink blush of it with the luminousness of an angel's skin.

The ensemble must have been favourable, for when he saw her Evan smiled in approval. To her, he looked as he had the night they'd first met, like a dream come true. And as he had that night, he was smiling at her as if he had been waiting all his life to meet her.

'Your second London ball,' he said, helping her into the carriage.

'I don't think the first one should count,' she replied. 'I was not there for very long.'

'Even though you were the guest of honour,' he reminded her. 'And we did not dance.'

'I danced with Alex,' she reminded him, and was surprised to see a shadow cross his face. 'It did not go well,' she added.

His mood instantly improved. 'It will be better this time, with me. We must waltz.'

'I would like that,' she said, staring out of the window and into the darkness. She hoped that he was right. If she failed at waltzing with her husband, it would be like displaying their marital problems for the whole *ton* to see.

But she needn't have worried. When they arrived at the ball, he introduced her to their hostess with a proud smile and gave no sign that they were not the happiest of newlyweds. Then he walked them to the dance floor and held out his hand to her.

She took it, and with a single tug she was in his arms. He swept her out onto the floor and in a moment they were spinning around the room. To her relief, they moved easily through the steps, as if they belonged together in a lover's embrace.

When they were close like this, his smile burned even brighter and she felt an answering glow on her own cheeks, which only intensified as he dipped his head to whisper in her ear, 'This is nice.'

As she nodded in response, she felt his breath moving against her cheek, almost like a tiny kiss. 'Wonderful,' she said on a sigh.

'Promise me you will never waltz with anyone but me,' he said, still so soft that no one else could hear. 'Save it for me, as you save yourself.'

'Yes.' His comparison between the dance and intimacy was both exciting and shocking. She could not believe that he would suggest such a thing in public, even if only she could hear. In reality, she could not believe that he said such things to her at all, for it was still hard to believe that they belonged together. Surely she had been destined for a man just a bit more ordinary.

But as they danced she caught a glimpse of the two of them in a large mirror on the opposite wall of the ballroom, and it seemed as if they belonged together. A splendid golden idol of a man and his equally splendid glittering bride.

And if that woman did not remind her of herself? Well, that had been the point of the new clothes, after all. And the new hair, and the pearls and feathers. To marry a duke, one needed to be a duchess, so that was what she must become.

And if she was as false as her diamonds? Then she must accept the fact that, to her husband, at least, appearances were more important than truth.

All too soon, the dance was over and he handed her off to her next partner, but not before planting a kiss on her knuckles to remind her to return to him.

It was the beginning of a perfect evening. She danced every dance, changing partners each time, surprised to find that many of the young men who partnered her were as dazzled by her company as she was by them.

But, through it all, she never forgot the presence of her husband, smiling at her in encouragement from across the room. When the time came to proceed to dinner, she was surprised to find that she was to be escorted by Alex and not Evan, who was seated just down the table from her.

'Are you enjoying the dancing this evening?' he asked with a playful smile. 'Or will you tell me the truth, that you would rather be at home with your copybook?'

She laughed. 'Copying graphs and equations is most diverting. But I must dance once in a while, if only to keep in practice.' Then she added, 'But today, when we left, I was in the middle of a book.'

'Let me guess,' he said, touching his temple. 'Trigonometry? Or was it calculus?'

'Probability,' she replied. 'It is very interesting.'

'Wherever did you find that in Evan's library?' he asked, surprised.

'Not in the library,' she said. 'I found it at Hatchards. A lady is expected to shop, after all. And I would much rather go to the bookshop than the modiste.'

'But probability,' he said, giving her an appraising look. 'Are you planning to take up gambling? It is an acceptable hobby for the wife of a duke. But only if you lose more than you can afford, so the gossips have something to put in the scandal sheets.'

'I suppose my purely theoretical interest is suspect,' she said with a sad shake of her head. 'I do not think I will ever understand the *ton.*'

'Take heart,' he said, 'the season cannot last for ever. Soon you will return to Fallon Court, where nothing ever happens.'

'It sounds delightful,' she said, smiling behind her hand.

'It is good that you think so,' he replied. 'My mother loathed it. She much preferred the London season.'

'And I suppose your stepfather the Duke took her to all the balls,' she said, trying to imagine them.

'On the contrary, they were rarely seen together,' Alex replied.

'They were not happy?' she said, surprised. There had been nothing in her husband's descriptions of his early life that had implied that.

'They were very happy. Simply not with each other,' Alex explained. 'By marrying him, she became a duchess and was invited to all the parties with all the best people. And he had her money.'

'Oh,' she said, trying not to shiver. It sounded very much like the marriage her father had hoped for her to have. But now that she had met Evan, she wanted so much more. 'And your mother did not like Fallon Court?'

'She usually remained in London when the family returned to the country,' he said.

'How strange,' she replied.

'We did not find it so at the time,' he said, seemingly surprised at her interest.

'You did not remain with her?'

He shook his head. 'I went with the Duke. And with Evan, of course.' He glanced at her speculatively. 'You will find the library at the manor superlative.'

'I look forward to enjoying it,' she said, trying not to think of the poor motherless boys, at the mercy of a father who could be by turns demanding and neglectful. If and when she had children, she wanted better for them than that.

'Evan said that his father gave him much guidance so that he might become a successful peer.'

'The damned rules,' Alex said with a knowing nod. 'And I suppose you are expected to follow them as well. Fortunately, I was free of them and have been able to make my own way. I was a stepson, you see. That is even worse than being a second son. I hardly signified in the eyes of the Duke.'

'You missed the attentions of a father,' she said.

'You are mistaken,' he said with a shake of his head. 'I did not miss them at all. I was fed and clothed and that was sufficient. And by watching the old Fallon, I learned the things I did not want to do.' He smiled. 'If and when I have a son, I will not be as rigid with him as the Duke was with Evan.'

She glanced down the table to where her husband sat and wondered if having his father's example to live by had been a help or a hindrance.

As if he realised that they spoke of him, he raised his glass in toast to her and took a long, slow sip of his wine.

At the sight of his eyes burning into hers and the wetness of his closed lips as they rested on the glass, she forgot her concern for his past and thought only of the future. When he looked at her as he was now, it was as if champagne bubbled in her veins and rushed to her head. The room seemed unaccountably warm. Her dress, which had been as light as cobwebs when she'd put it on, now seemed heavy and cumbersome and she longed for the freedom that bed would bring.

It was a scandalous thought. She was blushing in

earnest now, and she had the strange feeling that Evan knew what he had done to her. As he looked at her, his smile changed to one of satisfaction and he took another sip of wine.

Next to her, Alex laughed. 'It seems there is one lesson he did not take from his father, and I am glad of it. He has learned how to keep his wife content and at his side.'

She blinked and turned back to him, surprised. 'What do you mean by that?'

'Only that you make a charming couple, and that, despite a few glaring differences, you are very well suited.'

'Thank you,' she said, relieved that he would say so.

'And as far as those aforementioned differences,' he said with a secretive smile, 'there is someone here that I am sure you would very much like to meet. I will make the introductions after dinner.' Then he turned to talk to the lady on his other side, leaving her in suspense.

When the meal ended and the dancing began again, Alex pulled her away to a corner of the room, where a lady sat, staring out at the dancers with a faintly disapproving air.

'Annabella,' Alex said in a scolding tone. 'Alone again.'

She responded with a sardonic smile. 'My husband and his set abandoned the party almost before the dancing began. Since I do not favour whatever vice he is currently engaging in, I decided to remain.'

Alex laughed, although it was hard to tell from the lady's expression whether the comment was meant in jest or in seriousness. 'Well, it is your good fortune that you are here. I have someone who shares a common interest with you.' Then he glanced to Maddie. 'Your Grace, the Duchess of Fallon, may I present Lady Byron?' He looked back to the seated woman with an encouraging smile. 'I thought, with your similar interest...'

'I fear many women share a common interest with me,' she said with a frown. 'Tell me you did not bring me another devotee of my husband, for I have no desire to discuss his habits or his poetry.'

Maddie shook her head. 'While poetry is very nice, I find I much prefer the analytical to the literary. Mathematics, in all forms, fascinates me.'

Lady Byron's prim demeanour was replaced with an eager smile, and she patted the seat beside her. 'By all means, come sit beside me then. I adore it as well. It is so good to find someone with similar interests, is it not? So many women of late cannot see beyond their own noses when it comes to such matters.'

'I wonder if it would be possible to change that?' Maddie said, a plan forming in her mind. 'I certainly wish to expand my knowledge with current texts, but I am experiencing a difficulty lately. I don't suppose you read French?'

'Why do you ask?'

'I have a calculus book that needs translating, and while the subject is within my grasp, its language is a bit beyond me,' she admitted.

'I know just the one,' Lady Byron said with a nod. '*An Elementary Treatise on the Differential and Integral Calculus.* I have Mr Babbage's translation already in my possession.'

'How exciting,' Maddie replied.

'I will lend it to you, if you pay a call on me tomorrow morning.'

'I would be honoured,' she said, unable to contain her excitement. 'I had thought I would have to struggle through the pages one word at a time. But to have a translation…'

Lady Byron smiled. 'You will find it illuminating, I assure you.'

'I thought the two of you would get on well together,' Alex said, backing away. 'I will leave you to your discussion, then.'

And so he left them alone, and Maddie passed the rest of the evening talking of proofs and probability, hardly noticing when the musicians stopped playing and the guests began to call for their carriages.

When she found her husband exiting the card room, her face was still flushed with the excitement of intellectual stimulation.

He glanced down at her with a curious smile. 'Who has put such a pretty blush on your cheeks, my dear? Let me know the man, and I will call him out for flirting with you.'

'No one in particular,' she said, not wanting to reveal such a mundane source of excitement.

'Not telling? Never mind then,' he said with a knowing nod. 'I will make you forget him.'

When the Fallon brougham arrived, Evan helped her up into her seat and climbed in beside her, sitting so close that his thigh pressed against her skirt. She could feel the heat of his body through the silk, and once again she felt the urge to strip bare and let the night air cool her. A tremor went through her body.

In response, he chuckled. Then he dropped an arm over her shoulder and pulled her into his lap.

'What are you doing?' she said, shocked.

'What I wanted to do all evening,' he said, wrapping his arms around her. 'I am holding my wife in my arms as I did when we waltzed. Do you mind?'

She thought for a moment and smiled. 'We cannot dance in a carriage.'

'Perhaps not,' he agreed. 'But you might be surprised at the things we can do, if the ride is long enough.'

Surely he could not be suggesting what she thought he was suggesting. Not with the carriage driver and grooms and all of London just outside the doors.

He laughed. 'I have made you blush.'

'How can you tell in the dark?' she said, sure that he was right.

He laid the back of his hand against her cheek. 'You feel warm to me.' Then he dropped the same hand to cup her right breast. 'Yes. You are definitely flushed.'

She gasped.

His hand tightened imperceptibly. 'Do you want me to stop?'

'No,' she said in a whisper.

'Good,' he replied, sounding smug in the darkness. Then he settled his other arm about her waist. 'I think I would like to kiss you as well.'

Perhaps she'd had too much wine, but this sounded like a deliciously dangerous idea. She closed her eyes and puckered her lips in preparation.

He laughed again, and bussed her on the lips, which was surprisingly disappointing. Then he said, in a voice that raised the hair on her arms, 'Relax.' She was not sure if it was a request or a command, but she was helpless to refuse.

This time, when he kissed her, he covered her mouth softly with his own, breathing her breath and returning it mingled with his own. 'Better?' he murmured against her mouth.

'Better,' she agreed, smiling.

'Then let me do it again,' he said, and his tongue pressed against the seam of her lips, then slipped between them. This time, the kiss did not end, but went on and on until her breast felt hot beneath his hand and her body trembled, making her lean into him for warmth and support. His tongue was moving in her mouth now, as if hinting at the love-making that would happen between them, and her breath caught and released on a sigh as a strange heat surged through her.

He sensed the change in her and he paused the kiss, making her moan in disappointment. 'So sweet,' he murmured against her cheek. 'Sweet and beautiful.'

She pulled away in surprise, peering into the darkness and trying to read the expression on his face.

'Has no one told you that you are beautiful?' he said, leaning back as well.

'My mother said I was pretty enough,' she admitted, a little embarrassed.

'I should have told you before,' he replied, nuzzling her throat. 'We married so quickly. If I had courted you properly, you would have known.'

'You would have flattered me,' she said with a sigh.

'Is it flattery if it is the truth?' he asked, pulling away to look into her eyes.

'I do not know,' she said. 'I have no experience in such things.'

He laughed. Then he lowered his head to kiss her again, this time on the chin and throat, and even lower until his mouth reached the swell of her breast.

Shocked, she tried to tug her bodice up to hide the bare skin.

He raised his head again and looked into her eyes. 'There are many things that you do not know. This is one of them.' Then, very gently, he pulled her hands away from the fabric and tugged the bodice down again, until it rested even lower than it had before. 'I like your breasts,' he said in a very matter-of-fact tone. 'I would like to see more of them. And touch them. And kiss them.' Then he gave her an expectant look.

'Now?' she said, barely able to breathe at the thought.

'If you do not mind,' he said. Then he smiled. It was the sort of smile that would make a smart woman foolish, and she was sure that he knew the effect it created in her.

Despite that, her instinct was to say no. But then she remembered that she was married, and she had promised herself that she would no longer refuse him. Still, there had been nothing in her mother's little speech that covered the romantic etiquette of carriages.

Now, her husband looked like he was about to laugh. He dragged a coaxing finger along the edge of the bodice, touching her so lightly that she shivered.

'Is that a yes?' he asked.

Unable to speak, she nodded.

'Good. Because your dress is cut devilishly low and I have been thinking about this moment all night.' Then his fingers slipped inside her stays and eased her breasts up until they crested the top of her gown and lay exposed in the moonlight.

Her nipples tightened, in part from the cool night air, but mostly because he was touching them, brushing them gently with his fingers and pausing to pinch each in turn.

His smile was softer now, as if he had just been surprised with a gift. 'Lovely,' he said on a sigh. 'Just as I knew they'd be.'

The comment brought out a strange feeling in her. Pride. She had seen them all her life and had never thought one way or the other about her breasts. But now she looked down at them, surprised at his response, eager to see them through his eyes.

Experimenting, she arched her back and thrust them forward.

His expression changed to something hot and hungry and not totally in control. Then his mouth came down on a nipple and he sucked.

For a moment the world seemed to stop around her, the noise of the carriage and the traffic outside dwindled to nothing and all she could hear was the sound of their breathing, his deep and even, hers fast, gasping in shock.

There had definitely been nothing about this in her mother's lecture. For one thing, they were not in the bedroom, and for another, there was enough light in the carriage that she could see exactly what he was doing to her, and the way her body was responding. Her nipple, when he released it to minister to the other, was tight and still glistening with the wetness of his kiss. Her thighs felt wet as well. Her entire body was eager for his kiss, his touch, and the final confusing thrust and rush of his body into hers.

He toyed with her for a while, then looked up into her surprised face and smiled. 'Do not worry. I know there is not enough room or comfort to love you properly in a carriage. And it is very late.' He glanced at his watch and swore. 'The whole house will be up by the time we are home. Perhaps tomorrow…'

She could not even manage a response to this. For though he must know far more about what was possible in a carriage than she did, his promise to wait went against her untested instincts, and the need to do something now and quickly before the feeling faded again.

So she grabbed him by the cravat and pulled his lips to hers to ask, no, to demand one last kiss. He gave it willingly, opening her lips again and thrusting deep into her mouth in possessive strokes, and palming her breasts, pushing her back into the carriage seat so she could not escape from him, even if she wanted to.

Then, without warning, something in her seemed to break, like the dawn. She was shaking against him, gasping and whimpering, no longer in control of her mind or her body.

He seemed to know what was happening, for he gave one last forceful thrust with his tongue, then withdrew to let her breathe, soothing her with gentle kisses on her jaw, before pulling her dress back into place to hide the evidence of their play.

'We are home,' he whispered, stroking a stray curl out of her face and giving her a satisfied smile before pushing her back on the seat and straightening her skirts for her.

Then the grooms were opening the carriage door for her and the moment had ended.

Chapter Ten

As Evan took his usual seat by the fire at White's, he considered the possibility of a nap. A man of his age should not be dozing in public in the middle of the day. But it had been a long night with little sleep, and he certainly hoped he would have no sleep again tonight.

He could not contain his grin at the prospect of spending the evening with a wife who would be more than willing, after the delightful interlude in the carriage.

He smiled to himself at the memory of it. He had never been with a virgin before, but had been told that the first experience was often painful and awkward and devoid of pleasure for both parties. But no one had mentioned the joy of discovery that might accompany it. It had been clear last night that, while Maddie had been afraid of the marital act, she'd known nothing of the pleasure that it might entail. Now that she'd had a taste of that, there would be no more difficulties.

If, that was, he had the strength to keep up with her. After a surreptitious glance around him, he settled back into his chair and closed his eyes.

'Fallon!'

He snapped awake again, annoyed to see his father-in-law heading for the empty seat at his side.

'Goddard,' he grunted in acknowledgement, wishing the fellow would go to the devil and leave him alone. After the wedding, Evan had presented him with the introductions to places and people that he'd requested and had hoped that would be enough. Apparently, the man intended to socialise with him as well.

'Thank you so much for the invitation to your club. I have been trying to get into White's for some years but needed the right man to put me forward for membership.'

'You're welcome,' Evan said, thoroughly regretting that he had done the man a courtesy.

'It is so good to be here with you. And I understand Glenmoor is a member as well.' When there was no response, he continued, 'I trust my daughter is not giving you any trouble.' To this, he added a knowing laugh that danced on Evan's last nerve.

'Trouble?' Evan repeated. Maddie at her worst could not cause too much trouble. If anything, her timidity was the problem, and her father was the cause of that. 'None that I am aware of.'

'That is good to know. I raised her to be obedient,' Goddard said with a toothy grin that set Evan's own teeth on edge. 'That is why it surprised me to hear she was running with Byron and his crowd.'

'What?' Evan sat up straight in his chair, wondering if he had somehow nodded off into a nightmare.

'She was seen going into his house, just today,' Goddard said, clearly enjoying the fact that he knew more than Evan. 'I did not think you were the sort to allow her such rackety companions.'

The gall of the man. He had not cared one whit the sort of fellow his daughter married. Now he dared criticise the way their marriage was run. He gave Goddard a steely look and replied, 'I trust my wife to make her own decisions and am sure that there is a logical reason for her presence in that house.'

'Are you sure that is wise?' the other man replied with a smirk. 'When she was in my home, I allowed no such foolishness.'

'Since she is not in your home any more, your opinion hardly matters,' Evan responded. Then he thought of the way Maddie had reacted on their wedding night, trembling and cringing when he came to her room, in terror of his displeasure. 'What is more, when she was under your care, you achieved the obedience you are so proud of by beating it into her.'

'I only struck her when necessary,' Goddard blundered on, impervious to his disapproval. 'It is unwise to let women get the upper hand in a household, or chaos reigns.'

Evan took a long, slow sip of his whisky, considering his answer to this. His father had often said that a man was made or broken by the company he kept. If it weren't for the connection of marriage, he would not give this uncouth and violent man the time of day. 'In my experience, it is never necessary to hit a woman,' he said at last.

Goddard laughed. 'Then your experience cannot be very great. You have barely been married two weeks, after all.'

'To a girl so eager to get away from you that she was climbing the walls of my garden,' he finished, glaring at the man.

Apparently, some of his displeasure was finally

getting through Goddard's thick skin, for he gave a nervous laugh. 'I made sure she did not do that twice. I locked her in her room until the wedding.'

That did much to explain the poor girl's terror in the church, and her behaviour after. 'You had to force her to marry me.'

'She should not have needed to be forced,' Goddard said, shaking his head. 'If Madeline had any common sense, she'd have married you without my prodding.'

'And if you had any common sense, you'd have given her some say in her future,' he replied, feeling rage rising within him. 'And now you think to parlay her rise in station into a better position for yourself.'

'That is the whole point of marriage,' the other man said. 'It is an arrangement to benefit both families involved. I notice you did not think twice about taking the dowry offered when you wed her.'

It was true. He had given as much thought to the land that would change hands as he had the need to silence any scandal concerned with their strange meeting. And he certainly had not bothered to ask her for her hand or her opinion. The whole matter had been settled without her input.

And now it appeared that she might be running

wild with Byron and his lot. Perhaps that was what she had wanted all along. It made him wonder if he knew her at all. But he certainly knew and disliked her father, and it was time to put the man in his place. 'Perhaps you thought to buy my co-operation with a few acres of land, but I agreed to help you before I knew how you treated your daughter. I have invited you here and introduced you to my friends. But after this conversation, do not expect me to put you up for membership. I will not cut you in the street, but beyond that, sir, I will have no responsibility for your future. Improve your manners, and make what you can of our connection, but do it without my help.' Then he rose from his chair and left the club to go home to talk to his wife.

It had been the best day in recent memory. Perhaps the best day of her life. Maddie smiled, hugging the translated book to her side as she exited the Fallon carriage and skipped the few steps to her front door.

In Lady Byron, or Annabella, as she now called her, she had found a kindred spirit who was able to talk with her on matters more weighty than the latest styles from Paris. The lady had been tutored by a Cambridge professor, and was equally well versed in literature, philosophy and the sciences. She was the most engaging conversationalist that Maddie had ever met.

She was also unhappy in her marriage, poor thing. It seemed that her husband, though he had charmed a wide swathe of London society, was not an easy man to live with. Maddie felt quite sorry for her and hoped that her visit had done something to lift her spirits.

She was barely across the threshold when she heard her husband calling from the study. 'Madeline!'

She could not help the little start it gave her, for it was a surprise to find him home so early, with several hours before dinner. There was also no trace in his tone of the affection he had shown last night, or even at breakfast this morning, when he had called her Maddie and poured her chocolate for her.

She set the book on the entrance hall table with her reticule and hurried down the hall to see what was wrong.

When she arrived in the doorway, he looked up from the bills that were scattered across his desk and said, 'Home at last.' He was watching her intently, as if waiting for her to reveal some secret.

'And you are here early,' she said brightly, deciding to ignore the tension and do her best to return things to normal.

'Come in. And shut the door behind you,' he added with a stern look.

She did as she was told, then took a seat in front of his desk, balancing nervously on the edge of the chair and waiting for him to speak.

'When I was at the club, I met your father. He wanted to talk of you and the friends you are making, since our marriage.'

'Oh,' she said, hoping that he did not notice her flinch. It would be bad enough to be lectured over something she had control over, but there was nothing she could do about her father and his lack of society graces.

'I spoke to him about his treatment of you in the past and expressed my displeasure.'

'Oh,' she said, surprised that he would bother, since they had never really discussed the matter. Had he guessed how bad it had been and wanted to avenge her? She wished he would not, for the whole matter was better forgotten. 'Thank you,' she added, hoping that they could drop the subject and get back to the mood he had been in that morning.

'If, in the future, he does not treat you with the utmost respect, you must tell me immediately.'

'Of course,' she said automatically, knowing that she would not. She would never have the nerve.

'In addition, I have told him that our marriage does not give him carte blanche to our social circle or our home. If you wish to see him I will not stop you. He is your relative, after all. But I would prefer not to be at home for him.'

'As you wish.' Her father would be irate, of course. But that did not matter. If her husband did not want to see him, she was not about to argue.

'I am pleased to find you so understanding,' he said. 'But that is not the only reason I wished to speak to you.'

'Oh,' she said, unsure of what else she might have done to displease him, other than to be related to Mathew Goddard.

'What were you doing visiting Lord Byron?' he asked, his frown deepening.

There was an apology ready on her lips almost before he'd got the question out. But she stopped it, confused. What had she done that was in any way more objectionable than paying a morning call, as all the other ladies of her set did?

'I was not visiting Lord Byron,' she said, giving him an encouraging smile. 'I was visiting his wife. I met her when we went to the Dowager Duchess of Wainstaff's ball last night. Alex introduced us,' she added, hoping that would make things clearer.

'He did.' By the flat delivery of the words, it sounded as if she had made things worse, not better. 'I will have to thank him for that.'

'It was very kind,' she said, ignoring the dark undercurrent of those words.

'And you did not see Lord Byron at all on this visit?'

'Of course not,' she said with a nervous laugh. Surely she did not need to count their passing in the hallway as she'd entered.

He gave her a critical look. 'You are not telling the whole truth, are you?'

'I saw him just for a moment,' she corrected. 'He was on his way to the door. He greeted me and was gone.'

'And your visit with his wife?'

'Was purely social, I assure you. I wanted to borrow a book of hers.'

'Because I do not want you associating with that poet.' He said the final word as if poetry was something vile.

'His wife is not the least bit poetical,' she assured him with a smile. 'She is a most sensible woman. Very studious. We discussed mathematics.'

'Mathematics,' he said, as if it was something worse than poetry.

'As I said, I borrowed a book from her.'

'If that is all,' he said with a dubious sigh. 'And you say Alex encouraged this meeting?'

'We sat next to each other at dinner,' she reminded him.

'You seem to spend a lot of time talking to him,' he said, as if he had discovered something she should be ashamed of.

'I thought you wanted me to treat him as family.' She was surprised at the change in his opinion.

'And I did not think you would take the words to heart as you have,' he said.

'Do you wish me to avoid him?' She held her breath, hoping that the answer was no. She had few enough friends and did not want to lose the ones she had just made.

Her husband sighed, and pinched the bridge of his nose between two fingers. Then he dropped his hand and looked at her again. 'No, that would not do either. I simply want you to be sensitive to the fact that people might talk if you are too much in his company.'

'That is ridiculous,' she blurted out, shocking herself with her boldness. But it had sounded almost as if he thought she was harbouring some tendre for his brother.

'You really do not understand the *ton* at all, do you?' he said, shaking his head.

'I do not,' she agreed. 'It seems to me, no matter what I do, you tell me that it has resulted in people talking about me. Would it be better if I talked to no one and never left the house?'

'Then you would appear to be a recluse,' he said with a fleeting smile.

'And appearances are everything,' she replied, thoroughly depressed by the fact.

He nodded. 'As a duchess, you are the epitome of English womanhood.'

'Then I fear you will never be happy with me,' she said, 'for I have been trying to do everything you've asked of me.'

'All but the thing that wives are most expected to do,' he reminded her softly, looking at her with an expression that she had never seen before. He still seemed angry, and for a moment she wondered if he would strike her, as her father used to.

But he made no move. He was waiting for her to answer his last comment. But the statement made no sense in the current context. It was not as if she could do anything about the matter here. 'It is day-light,' she blurted, confused.

'It is,' he agreed, and there was that fleeting smile again.

Her mother had said it would be dark. And in a bedroom. 'We are in your study.'

'And last night we were in a carriage,' he reminded her.

'A moment ago you were angry with me,' she reminded him.

'And there is no quicker way to return me to good humour,' he said. Then he got up from his desk and walked to the door. The key turning in the lock was a deafening click in the silence of the room.

He walked back to her chair then, standing behind her, his hands on her shoulders as they had been on the night he had given her the false necklace. He pressed down upon them and began a gentle massage of the tight muscles. 'As I was saying before, you spend far too much time talking with my brother.'

'Oh,' she said as his hand slid down her arm to take her hand and pull her out of the chair.

'I worry that you have more in common with him than you do with me.'

'I don't really think...' she murmured. And she

didn't think. Couldn't think. For in one rough movement he had swept the papers on his desk off onto the floor.

'I think it is time we found a common interest,' he said, grabbing her by the waist and lifting her to sit on the empty desk. Then he leaned forward and took her lower lip between his teeth, tugging on it ever so gently.

She shuddered, her hands clutching at the edge of the desktop on either side of her skirts as he reached down to grab her knees, pushing her legs apart to step between them.

'Eh?' she said, for it was all she could manage around the tantalisingly rough kiss.

He released her mouth and whispered in her ear. 'You were surprisingly responsive last night. And all I did was kiss your breasts. Let us see what happens when I touch you somewhere else.' His hands slid from her knees, down her calves to the hem of her skirts. He raised them, rolling them out of the way to pool in her lap.

His palms were resting on the tops of her thighs, just at the place where her stockings ended, fingers tracing the garters and the cool flesh just above them. 'Today, I think I shall take you just like this, without even ruffling your gown. Tonight, I will unwrap you like a gift and play with you at my leisure. But for now?' His hands moved higher, to the crease where her legs ended, and his thumbs…

He nipped the side of her throat as his thumbs pressed into the folds of her body and entered her. 'I will be gentle at first,' he assured her, his teeth still grazing the cords of her neck. 'As befits your innocence, which I mean to despoil right here on my desk.'

'Oh, dear.' His words were rude and undignified and, to her surprise, almost as arousing as his fingers, which were dipping in and out of her, and had found a spot that made her tremble each time he touched it.

'I will be gentle until you are begging me to take you harder,' he said, nibbling on her earlobe, whispering the words. 'But you must do so very quietly, for it is broad daylight and anyone could be listening at the door. I can make you scream with pleasure if I like, or I can let you be the quiet little mouse you so often are.'

His fingers stopped their ministrations and suddenly he took her wrists, encouraging her hands to come to the fastenings of his breeches, and as she undid them she closed her eyes, afraid of what she would see.

'Look at me,' he whispered. 'Look down. It is daytime and you can see everything I am doing to you.' He cupped her sex with one hand and took himself in the other, leaning forward until the two almost met. 'Do you want me to do that?'

'Yes,' she whispered.

'Even if it hurts?'

'Please,' she begged.

'Even if you scream?'

'Oh, God,' she moaned, staring down at the hard length of him as he eased forward and took her inch by delicious inch. She was shaking, already close to begging, as he had said she would, and they had barely begun.

When he had come fully into her and she thought it was not possible to feel anything more, he began to move. Very slowly at first, one hand lazily stroking the place they were joined. Then the pace increased and with it the sensation, like breaking waves in a storm.

She wanted to move with him, to ease the pressure building inside her. But he controlled all, doling out pleasure to her a little at a time until…

He was right. She wanted to beg. She wanted to scream. To pound at his chest and demand the release that she was sure must be coming. For if it didn't she would die, right here, spread on his desk like a sacrifice on an altar. She grabbed his lapels, fisted them in her hands and uttered the only word she could think of, 'More!'

And he laughed at her. Or perhaps with her, she was not sure. But he gave her what she wanted, which was all that mattered. He moved faster, harder, deeper, pressing his lips into her throat as if at any minute he might bite hard enough to mark her, to prove to everyone in the house that she belonged to him and him alone.

The thought finished her, and she sank her teeth into the collar of his coat, blocking her rising scream with the wool as her body caught and shook and her hips bucked against him.

His hands clutched her by the bottom, holding her steady as he poured himself into her, shaking as his iron control shattered and he was spent.

They sat there for a moment in silence, leaning against each other for support, until their breathing returned to normal and their lust cooled. Then he reached for a handkerchief, gently wiping away the evidence of their lovemaking and rearranging her skirts, until they hung as straight and un-mussed as he'd promised. Then he held out a hand to help her down from the desk.

When her feet touched the floor, her legs buckled under her, still weak from passion.

He caught her easily against him, kissing her until she regained her strength to stand on her own. Then he said, 'Shall I visit you in your rooms tonight? A bed might not be an exotic location for sport, but you will find it is more comfortable than a desk for some of the things I wish to do with you.'

She had meant to escape this room before revealing her shock at what they had done together just now. But the idea that there were things still to learn undid her, as did the casual way he announced that her next lesson would be tonight. She was blushing furiously, not just on her cheeks but over every inch of her body.

'Close your mouth, Maddie,' he said with a grin. 'Or I will give you a good reason to be shocked, and I do not have time for that right now. It is broad daylight, as you noted before, and there is still work to be done before supper.'

'Of course, Your Grace,' she said, then amended, 'Evan.' Then she hurried from the room.

She was only a few steps down the hall when she saw Mr Ramsey coming towards her from the other side of the house. Good God, she did not want to see him now. What if he guessed what had just happened? Surprisingly, the thought made her want to laugh, which seemed even more inappropriate than making love on a desk.

'Your Grace,' he called, his pace increasing to reach her before she could escape up the stairs.

'What is it, Mr Ramsey?' She struggled to maintain her composure, glancing longingly past him to the front hall and the book she had abandoned there.

'I see you were coming from the study. Have you had the chance to speak to your husband about what we discussed last week?'

She had no intention of telling the man how little talking had been done during her recent visit with her husband, though he might guess if he noted her blush. 'Our discussion?' she said, struggling to remember what it was that the man had wanted.

'About control of your trust,' he reminded her.

'Ah, yes,' she said, searching for an excuse. 'My husband was in no mood to talk about money just now. Perhaps another day.'

'As I told you before, the matter is quite vital. In fact, the urgency increases by the minute.'

She frowned, wondering if her husband was aware of the difficulties at all. He certainly had not seemed bothered. Not about money, at least. 'Have you spoken to him about the problems yourself?

Surely you would be better able to educate him on the subject than I.'

'He has made his opinions known and I would not dare contradict him,' the man said, looking at her with the beginnings of impatience. 'But you have influence. And it is your money, after all.'

'It is,' she agreed. What had he said when they had spoken of her money? That he did not want the obligation until she fully trusted him. He had meant with her body, which was a matter they had just settled.

But did she trust him with her money?

She thought of the false necklace and the fact that he had not yet admitted to it. Perhaps things were worse than even Mr Ramsey thought. If she wanted the whole story, she would have to find a time to look at the ledgers again and read the truth for herself. 'I will do my best,' she said. 'But I must wait until the time is right.'

'And when will that be?' he replied, reaching out to touch her arm.

Surprised at the contact, she pulled away. 'I will tell you as soon as I have talked to him. Until that time, do not bother me again.'

Then she hurried past him, grabbed her book and went up the stairs to her room.

Chapter Eleven

It had been three weeks since his wife's visit to Lord Byron's house, and the subsequent interlude on the desk, and all the interludes after that. Evan could not help but grin, thinking of his nightly visits to his wife's bed. It was not as if he had expected them to be unpleasant. But after her initial resistance to lying with him, he had not expected her to be such an enthusiastic lover.

Since their first time together he had come to her every night, and each night she had smiled at him as if he'd hung the moon, opening her heart to him in a way that no mistress ever had. It had aroused him in ways other than the physical. For the first time in his life, he understood why poets went on and on about love.

The feeling would be transitory, of course. He would get back to his old self, sooner or later. He hoped it was sooner. His father had always said that strong and passionate emotions, particularly those of a romantic nature, were unhealthy. Love clouded the mind and made a reasonable man into a fool, affecting his judgement and leading to irrational behaviour.

If the way Evan felt lately was any indication, his father had been right. He was happy, of course. But the joy was mixed with a vulnerability he did not understand. When he was with Maddie, he felt too exposed, like one of those sea creatures that needed a shell to survive and only poked their heads out for a limited time before retreating to the safety of their home.

Eventually, he would have to come to his senses. But for the moment, each day was exciting in a risky sort of way, like walking on the edge of a cliff and looking out on a vista he had never seen before.

He greeted his wife at breakfast with a smile and a kiss, and the good mood that remained after the excellent night's sleep that had followed even more excellent lovemaking.

She, on the other hand, looked paler than usual. While she accepted the kiss with a wan smile, she said nothing, remaining as quiet as she had been when they'd first met.

He observed her as she stared down into her tea-cup, trying to decide if he had done or said something that would spoil her mood. Was this the beginning of the end of the honeymoon?

He noticed that her plate was empty. It was possible that she was merely hungry. Or perhaps she was avoiding food, as she had on the first day of their marriage, when she had been unsure of everything about her new life, including him. On that day he had coaxed her to eat, and he would do so again.

He took the plate of kippers and pushed it down the table towards her with an encouraging smile.

Without a word, she rushed from the breakfast table, her hand covering her mouth.

When she came back a short time later, she was even paler, and reached for her cup with trembling fingers.

'My dear,' he murmured, reaching out a hand to steady hers. 'Are you all right?' It was an idiotic question, for clearly she was not. But he had always felt helpless in the face of illness and had no idea what he might do to make it better. 'Shall I summon a physician?'

To his surprise, the housekeeper, who had followed her back into the dining room, gave a contemptuous sniff at the suggestion. Then she stepped forward and removed the tray of kippers from the table, passing it to a footman and giving Evan a dark look, as though he was somehow at fault for what had just happened.

Without waiting for a request or permission, she poured out a cup of tea for the Duchess and placed a piece of dry toast on her empty plate. Then she laid a motherly hand on Maddie's shoulder, ignoring the impropriety of such a familiar gesture. 'Small bites, Your Grace. A woman in your condition needs nourishment, no matter how hard it is to take.'

'My condition?' Maddie said, confused.

The housekeeper gave her another pitying look. 'It is early yet. But I think congratulations are in order.'

'But I have not even missed my courses,' Maddie said, blushing furiously as she looked at him. 'I am late. But only a week. That is really no time at all.'

'It is enough,' the housekeeper said.

Pregnant. He should have known it was a possibility. That was the expected result of what they had been doing. But he had imagined, against all logic, that it would not happen right away, perhaps not for months or years. Perhaps not at all. His father had married twice and yet Evan was his only issue. Sometimes, even if one wanted children, none would appear.

But not this time. Not to him. He laughed. He could not help the joyous bubbling feeling in his chest at the prospect.

Apparently, this was the wrong response. The two women stared at him with faintly accusatory expressions, as if he was to blame for the morning's chaos. And now his laughter was making it worse.

He stared back at the housekeeper, trying to remain respectfully sober, but unable to stop smiling. 'Are you sure? If she does not know...'

Mrs Miller nodded. 'I have more than enough children of my own to tell what the first months are like. For some women it takes no time at all, and they know.'

Maddie blinked, apparently still in shock, and then she ran from the table again, unable to stand the sight of her toast.

Evan's smile disappeared and he rose to follow her, wanting to do something, anything at all, that might ease his wife's discomfort. But Mrs Miller held up a staying hand, then set it upon his shoulder, pushing him gently back into his chair. 'Best to let her get through the next few minutes on her own. I will see to it that she gets to her room, and has a cup of tea, at least. She will be better by afternoon, and you can talk to her then.'

Maddie stared miserably down into the porcelain urn she had found in the morning room and waited for her stomach to settle again. The thing was a chinoiserie delicacy, painted in birds and flowers with a thin gilt line at the rim, and exactly the sort of thing she imagined a duchess would be sick into. No common crockery for her. In an emergency, only the best china would do. Like her new clothes and her new hobbies, it did not really suit her, but it certainly looked nice.

It had been nearly three weeks since she had seen her new friend Annabella Lovelace. Though they corresponded regularly, Maddie had not risked a second visit to the Byron household, for fear of another lecture from her husband on the need for discretion.

Though she was not sure that it was part of the problem, she had taken the book she had borrowed from Annabella and hidden it in the wardrobe in her room. She still spent her mornings studying it and working enigmas or copying formulas. But she did all that quietly and privately, not even discussing it with Alex.

She spent most afternoons painting watercolours or practising scales on the pianoforte. Her playing was almost as bad as her painting. But both were better than the stitching and embroidery she did each night when she retired to the sitting room with her husband. He often complimented her on her industry and remarked that he was proud of her accomplishments.

She smiled wryly at the thought as she set the bowl aside. He was lying, of course. Or perhaps he was blind and a little deaf. There was no way her artistic or musical talents were anything more than a waste of time to assure him that she did not spend the day pining at the window like a spaniel, awaiting his return.

There was only one new habit that she felt she was really succeeding at, and it was the one that had got her into this sorry state. Now that the sickness had stopped, she considered the odds that her condition was exactly what the housekeeper said it was. She was unsure exactly what it took to conceive, but when one rolled a die over and over, probability stated that one would see all the numbers sooner or later.

And they had rolled this particular die at least once a night since that day in the study. Sometimes more than once. And in positions and locations that were quite outside of the imaginings evoked by her mother's inadequate explanation.

It still surprised her that it had happened so soon and so easily. Or that it could make her feel so miserable. But sickness like this was one of the symptoms, a sign of the change in her body to make it accommodate the child that was coming. She suspected that the way her stays felt painfully tight was another sign.

If Mrs Miller was correct, and there was no reason to think that she was not, then this was proof that, as Duchess, she was able to do this one most important thing right. In less than a year she might be giving her husband the heir he wanted. She would have fulfilled the one thing on his father's list of rules and requirements that her husband could not do for himself. That had to make up for everything she was doing wrong.

And then Evan would love her.

The thought came to her suddenly, dropping into place like the missing piece of a puzzle, and making her feel sick in an entirely different way.

There was no question that Evan wanted her. He wanted her frequently and insatiably, just as she wanted him. She knew it by the way he smiled when he came to her and held her like he never wanted to let her go.

It was more than she'd ever hoped for in a marriage.

And yet it was not enough. Though he smiled roguishly, he did not look at her with the hope-filled, weightless feeling she felt when she looked at him. And though he seemed to share the bone-deep contentment she felt after they made love, while she lay in his arms wishing that the moment would never end, it always did. He would tire of it, sometimes in minutes and other times in hours, but he would always pull away and return to his room, leaving her alone in hers.

It made her suspect that, while she could no longer imagine a life without him, he was quite capable of surviving without her.

And as for the words she hoped to hear? She did not have the nerve to be the first to say 'I love you' for fear that she would also be the last to say it. What would she do if the declaration was met with a puzzled smile or an awkward silence? Or, worst of all, suppose he patted her hand and explained that such things just weren't said by dukes and duchesses.

It was better to remain silent. This way she was

at least partially happy, as opposed to one hundred percent dissatisfied.

Hopefully, giving him a child would deepen the way he felt about her. He'd certainly seemed happy when she had left him in the dining room. She might yet hear him declare himself.

Just then Mrs Miller entered the room with a maid. Signalling the maid to take the basin, she set a cup of tea at Maddie's side. 'You will feel better after you drink this,' she said. 'It is ginger. If that does not help, we will try peppermint.'

'Thank you,' Maddie said, taking a cautious sip.

'When you feel well enough, I will take you up to your room, and bring you a light breakfast.'

'Very light,' said Maddie, taking another sip.

'And then, later, you may see His Grace again, and he will tell you how happy he is,' the woman said, draping a shawl around her shoulders and making her feel like an invalid. But it felt good to be spoiled and she allowed herself to be led upstairs, for toast and more tea and perhaps a nap.

Chapter Twelve

They were at another damned ball. Or so Evan had begun to think of them. It seemed that, at the height of the season, there was always some rout or drum or dance that required his attendance. And his wife's as well, for what impression would it give to go without her?

But was it really safe for her to be out and about? She had assured him, after frightening him very badly over the course of the last weeks, that she was only ill in the mornings and felt quite herself the rest of the time. And she could avoid the sickness altogether if she only nibbled at breakfast. She had even surprised him by taking the smoked herring with her supper, declaring herself voraciously hungry for the strangest things by evening.

Despite Mrs Miller's reassurance, he had called a surgeon, who had spent more time attending to

Evan than he had to his duchess, assuring him that he was not to worry about the current symptoms, which generally stopped in a month or two. After two glasses of brandy in the study, he had admitted that women often knew what was best for themselves and that his visit was unnecessary.

He worried all the same. He had spoken to Cook, reminding her that the lady of the house should have any delicacy she requested, no matter how costly. He had gone to Mrs Miller, cautioning her that his wife should not be overtaxed or bothered with household decisions that could just as easily be made by others. And lastly he had gone to Maddie herself, encouraging her to nap rather than bothering with morning calls, and wondering aloud if it would be better to cancel their planned engagements so she could rest in the evenings.

She had told him to mind his own business.

It was surprising, since she'd never dared to be so contrary. But the doctor had warned him that women were often short-tempered when pregnant and he must learn to be patient, just as he had at night, when he came to her room.

It had always been a sacrifice to leave her bed once the lovemaking was over. But he did not allow himself to give in to the urge to linger. It was better to leave her, and himself, wanting, more than to give in to decadence and lose control of the situation.

In his many rules on how one must behave as a duke, his father had given him the bare minimum of instruction on how to deal with the woman who would be his duchess. But he had been clear on one thing. He was to treat the future mother of his children with respect, and not burden her too much with his carnal desires. There were plenty of places in London where his needs could be met with discretion. Perhaps he should be visiting those and allowing his wife to have her rest.

But the idea gave him no pleasure. Despite what his father had encouraged, he could not manage to stay away from Maddie. It took little more than a shared glance to inflame him and she was just as bad. And there was definitely no stopping things once they had begun.

But really, what was the fun of restraint when in the bedroom? The only control he could manage was to return to his own room when the act was done, so that she could get the sleep that she and the baby must need.

She was coming towards him now, fresh off the dance floor on the arm of some young buck who was gazing at her besotted, as if he had any chance of getting further than a polonaise. She was wearing the rose-coloured gown that he liked, her pearls swinging against her breasts as she moved.

When she reached his side, she dismissed her partner with a polite thank you and turned to him, smiling. 'Are you enjoying your evening, Your Grace?'

'Of course,' he lied, not wanting to disappoint her. 'And you, my dear?'

'It is as delightful as always,' she said, smiling back at him.

'May I trouble you for a turn around the floor? I believe a waltz is about to begin.' He liked waltzing with her. It was the only thing that made these evenings bearable.

She shook her head. 'The next dance is a quadrille, and I do not think there is another waltz this evening. Perhaps we might dance when we are home.'

She was referring to their lovemaking, he suspected. He smiled and nodded. 'We most definitely shall.'

She glanced away from him to her next partner, who was approaching with a timid smile as if he feared to give offence to Evan.

He smiled back, trying not to be jealous. It was

clear she was as successful a duchess as he could have hoped for and that meant that she had to devote some of her attentions to dazzling the *ton*, just as his stepmother had. 'I will leave you to it, shall I?'

'If you must,' she said, still smiling.

'If you need me, I shall be in the card room.' But she wouldn't need him. She was quite fine on her own. It was surprisingly disappointing.

As Evan retreated and her next partner claimed her, Maddie smiled even more brightly, forcing herself to be as pleasant and accommodating as any woman in the room.

Her cheeks hurt from smiling. Her feet hurt as well, but she was not about to admit it to her husband, who was already treating her as if she were made of glass. If she told him she was the least bit tired, he would rush her home and insist on an early bedtime, with no visit that might disturb her rest.

When she was a girl, dreaming that she might have a London come out, she had never imagined that it would be possible to tire of balls. But she had. She was sick to death of them, and all similar obligations. But she was also aware that, while in London, they were expected to be sociable. Her job, if a duchess could be said to have employment, was to be just where she was, dancing and chatting and pretending to have a good time.

She would much rather be at home, alone with Evan. Or if she could not have his company, just at home alone. She had still not had time to finish the calculus book she had borrowed, and it had been at least a week since she'd had a letter from Annabella, who was probably at some other social gathering tonight, and as bored as she was here.

Lately, she had been far too busy to even think about maths. In her campaign to win her husband's heart, she had thrown herself into the kinds of activities he seemed to like, working to be the accomplished woman he had always expected to marry.

The house was filled to overflowing with cut roses, though in her delicate condition the scent was sometimes so overpowering that she had to leave the common rooms. But when she could stand them, she got out her sketchbooks and watercolours and committed their images to paper.

When she was not painting, she devoted herself to daily music lessons, consoling herself that it was merely another type of mathematics, with half and whole steps and hemi and semiquavers. It was an exercise in fractions, which was hardly complicated.

Or at least it should not be. So far, she had progressed no further than scales, and it was surprisingly hard to convince her fingers to move as the teacher wanted them to. She spent hours grinding through the notes, trying and failing to make the exercise sound as smooth and rhythmical as it had in the hands of the master.

When Evan had heard her, he had smiled, though it was clearly done to encourage her. 'The first lesson is the hardest. Or so I assume,' he had added to remind her that he had never needed one.

Then he'd taken over the keyboard and began to play a piece by Mozart from memory, his fingers flying over the keys with no effort at all. It made her wonder why she bothered. Surely a household did not need two skilled musicians. But her husband was a duke and had no time to play, whereas she had all the days of a lifetime to fill.

The evenings needed to be filled as well. So she kept dancing, smiling and making inane small talk where she pretended to be far more interested in the gossip of the day than she actually was. During a brief pause in the music she retreated to the ladies' retiring room, hoping for a quiet place where she might put her feet up for a moment and drop the façade. But tonight it was unusually full and the chatter louder than usual. So she retreated to a corner and reclined on a divan, allowing her eyes to drift closed and hoping that the others there would leave her alone.

Then the hubbub ebbed and she could not help overhearing the words of the woman nearest to her.

'Have you seen the latest issue of the *Ladies' Diary*?' one of them asked another. 'I swear I have no idea how to proceed on the newest enigma.'

'I could give you a hint, if you wish,' said another. 'I think I am very close to a solution.'

Maddie's eyes flew open and she sat up, turning towards the others to interrupt. 'You work the enigmas as well?'

There was a moment of shocked silence as the group recognised her, and then one woman admitted in a shy voice, 'Every chance I get.' Then she added in a conspiratorial tone, 'It is ever so much more diverting than doing needlework.'

'And knitting socks,' the second blurted out. 'I swear, if I make one more pair of those, I will run mad.'

Maddie laughed, clapping her hands together in excitement. 'I feared I was the only one to think thus. But then, I am just come from the country and had a very limited acquaintance there.'

'I expect things are quite different for you in London, Your Grace.' Then the other women fell silent, for they had not been introduced.

'And what are your names?' she asked, breaking the bounds of etiquette.

'I am Lady Crawford and my friend is Miss Penelope Verdan,' the first woman said. 'We are honoured to meet you, even more so now that we know you work the puzzles in the *Diary*. Tell me, have you figured out the matter in the latest one?'

Maddie smiled and nodded.

'Do not tell me.' Miss Verdan giggled. 'Once it is done, I will have no entertainment for the rest of the year.'

'Or you could try your hand at writing your own enigma,' Maddie said. 'I have done so on several occasions, but I have no one to test the problems on.'

'You could show them to us,' Lady Crawford said. And then covered her mouth quickly as she realised that she had just imposed her company on a duchess.

'Do not fear,' Maddie said, waving away her embarrassment. 'I have been longing for someone to suggest just that, but I did not know who might be interested.'

'If you would be so kind as to show us your work, there are at least a dozen ladies I know who would be eager to set their minds to a new problem,' Lady Crawford said.

'Tell me their names,' Maddie said, turning her dance card over and preparing to write. 'I will hold a salon of sorts at my home. We will have tea and cake and talk about the things that interest us, and there will not be an embroidery hoop or a knitting needle allowed.'

The women smiled and gave her a polite round of applause, and then began listing names. When they were finished, she had nearly a dozen names of women who thought similar to herself.

'I will send a round of invitations and, if it is convenient, we will meet on Wednesday morning, in my home,' she said. And then she offered them what felt like the first true smile she had given all evening.

Later that night, as Evan lay exhausted in his wife's bed, he dismissed his earlier worries that the evening had been too taxing for her. If anything, she seemed to have more energy tonight than she'd had recently and had loved him most enthusiastically, straddling him to ride out her orgasm, leaving him spent. He had never expected that his shy wife would become a temptress with a little coaxing.

She was lying beside him now, wearing nothing but a satisfied smile, skin passion-flushed in the firelight. When she noticed him watching her, she reached over to touch him lightly on the shoulder, as if to reassure herself that he was still there, and he returned the favour, nuzzling her neck and imagining her hovering over him, draped in jewels like some concubine.

The thought intrigued him. It was a fantasy that could easily be fulfilled with the help of a jewel case and a few silk scarves, and the thought made him hard again. 'Why do you never wear the diamonds I gave you?' he said, curling a lock of her hair around his finger and letting it spring back into place.

'Never?' she said with a laugh that seemed strangely nervous. 'We have hardly been together long enough to measure things in always and never.'

'Perhaps not,' he said, kissing her bare throat where the stones would lie. 'But you wore the pearls again tonight.'

'Because they match my gown,' she replied.

'But you have other gowns that would look well with diamonds,' he reminded her.

'The clasp is loose,' she said. 'I would not want to lose them.'

'Have you sent them to a jeweller for repair?' he

asked, running a finger from the side of her neck to the place between her breasts and then kissing the path that it had travelled.

'I will do so,' she said, rolling over onto her back and spreading her legs. 'Tomorrow.'

And then he rolled over onto her and forgot all about the question.

Chapter Thirteen

The next morning Maddie lingered over the first breakfast she had been able to eat in weeks. The nausea that had plagued her had passed as quickly as it had come, leaving her ravenously hungry, and with a craving for the kippers and eggs that had seemed so vile just a few days before.

Evan was not in the breakfast room when she came down and she wondered if, in her absence, he had changed his morning routine and had been eating in his room as well. She missed him. But the solitude gave her a chance to consider his question about the necklace on the previous evening.

The topic had brought her near to panic, for she had almost forgotten the problem of the false diamonds, and the hurt that she had felt on finding them. Now that she had his affection, it was far better than jewels. It did not matter any more, nor did she want to bother him with her discovery.

She had told a small lie that would buy her some time until she could decide what to do about the stone she had broken. It might be easiest to do exactly what she had told him she would, and take the necklace to a jeweller, asking him to replace the missing jewel with the same paste that the setting had contained. Then she would go back to wearing the necklace and be careful not to damage it in the future.

If she used her own money, there would be no receipt to prove the lie. After she made up the invitations to her mathematics salon, she would go to Bond Street and take care of the matter. Then there would be no reason to discuss it again.

As she helped herself to another cup of tea, Mr Ramsey entered the room, taking a seat on the opposite side of the table and filling his plate.

She had almost forgotten about the man, since she had been spending more time in her room during the daytime. But it was clear that he had not forgotten about her.

'Your Grace,' he said with a subservient smile.

'Mr Ramsey,' she replied, taking a mouthful of eggs so that she needn't say more.

'Have you had a chance to speak to your husband as of yet?' he asked, ignoring his own food to question her.

She chewed slowly, her mind searching for a response. But eventually she had to swallow. Then she said, 'I am sorry. The time has not been right.' In truth, she had not been thinking about it at all. Nor did she want to think of it now.

'You are aware that this matter is of the utmost importance,' he said, giving her a frustrated look.

'You have already told me so,' she replied, taking another bite of a breakfast that had suddenly lost its flavour.

'And there is no one in the house who would know better,' he added.

There was something about his assurance that annoyed her. But he was probably right. Before she could think of an answer, her husband appeared in the doorway, smiling broadly to see her there. 'Feeling better?' he asked.

'Much,' she agreed, relieved to have him there to interrupt.

But as he took his seat, his man of business spoke. 'We were just discussing the management of Her Grace's trust.'

'Really?' her husband said in a dry voice.

'She wishes to turn it over to you to manage,' Ramsey said with a firm nod in her direction.

But did she? Her mind raced. She could not remember ever saying those words specifically. She had agreed to talk to her husband about it, of course. When the time was right. And apparently the time was wrong, for she had been avoiding the issue for weeks.

Evan was looking at her now, expecting her to affirm what his man of business had just said. 'We were talking about it,' she agreed. That, at least, was perfectly true.

Her husband gave her a considering look. 'I am still not sure that it is a good idea. But it would simplify accounting, I suppose.'

It would simplify things because she would have no part in it. Right now, she had access to the bank whenever she wanted and could ask them about any activity. But from now on she would have to trust Mr Ramsey with the statements, and the paying of bills. And something about that felt very wrong.

'I will contact the bank and have the necessary papers drawn up,' Ramsey said, looking to her husband as if she wasn't even there.

'Leave them on my desk to be signed when you have them,' Evan said, then looked back to her. 'You honour me with your faith in my judgement. I will do my best to see that it is not misplaced.'

'Thank you,' she said, hoping that her answering smile did not look too nervous. After he had said such a loving thing, how could she tell him that she still had doubts? He would think that she did not trust him if she questioned him now.

With Ramsey there, it was not the private talk she would have preferred to have with Evan. And the man of business looked far too smug at his success. With a final grin in her direction, he angled his chair to face the Duke and began to talk of estate matters, cutting her out of further conversation.

After two days and several conferences with Ramsey, Evan still had his doubts about the man's plans for his wife's money. He kept emphasising the need for quick and decisive action and made the current state of the estate's financial affairs sound dire.

But surely the money from Alex had made some difference. Evan felt a total fool when tasked with balancing the ledgers, but he had been able to read the number on that cheque well enough and it had been close to a year's rental income on the whole of his property. Even if the crops were poor and the weather bad, there should be no problem for at least six months.

But to refuse the plan felt like a rejection of his wife's generous offer. He had told her they would wait until she fully trusted him before talking of money again. And at night he was sure she did.

In the daytime, it was another matter. Though she was agreeable and obedient, she was still nearly as quiet as she had been when they'd married. But she seemed happy enough. Or at least she did not seem as unhappy as she had been in those first days. And she was keeping busy, which was important.

When he'd asked her of her plans that morning at breakfast, she'd announced that she would be receiving callers at home today, which seemed a harmless enough activity, compared to her earlier visit to the Byron household.

He was on the way out of the house when the first woman arrived, and he was surprised to see that, rather than heading towards the receiving room as a normal caller would, she started up the stairs to the first floor, beaming and managing a curtsy as she passed him. 'Your Grace.'

'Madam,' he said with a puzzled smile and a bow. He did not recognise her as one of the wives of his friends, but that did not preclude her from being a guest of his wife's. He had no problem with her so-cialising with her own set, barring the earlier ex-ception.

But that did not explain why she was heading up the stairs towards the bedrooms. After greeting him, she continued on her way and another lady ap-peared in the hall, ready to follow after her.

'Your Grace,' she said with the same eager smile, curtsied in answer to his bow and then rushed past him as if she was late for an appointment.

Was his wife entertaining in her rooms in dis-habille? It was very French and not at all what he was expecting from the simple country girl he had thought he'd married. Still, it was not too objection-able as long as the company was not mixed. But he was curious as to what her reasoning might be for it.

Without a word, he turned and followed the last guest, watching as she turned down the hall and into the family wing. But, rather than entering the Duchess's rooms, she continued down the hall past them and went into the nursery suite.

Since there were no children in the house as yet, there was no reason for anyone to be there, much less a group of strange women. He stopped in the doorway of the classroom and saw that it was not just the two he had seen, but an entire room full of ladies, sitting at desks and tables with slates and chalk or with journals and pens, looking expectantly at his wife, who was standing at the front of the room, scribbling a mathematical equation on the slate board behind her.

At the sight of him she smiled shyly and stopped writing. 'Evan?'

'What are you doing?' he said.

'Nothing,' she said, then corrected herself. 'Nothing of interest, at least.' She meant of interest to him, he supposed. She was smiling again, as if to reinforce the innocence of what was going on.

'Would it not be more convenient to entertain on the ground floor?' he asked, staring at the group.

'This room is larger,' she supplied. 'There are so many of us, you see.'

'I see.'

'And I have ordered tea to be sent up,' she said, smiling again.

As if on cue, a servant appeared behind him in the hall, pushing a cart laden with teacups and biscuits.

'Well, if you are having tea I will not interrupt,' he said, baffled. And then he turned and walked away.

He pondered on the gathering for most of the

day, still wondering at the purpose of it, and at the large number of strange women who seemed to be giving Maddie their rapt attention. Had the whole world gone mad, or was it just him?

He was still thinking on it that afternoon, when he met Alex at White's. 'I do not understand my wife,' he said without preamble as his brother dropped into the chair at his side.

'Based on your lecture to me the night I met her, I did not think that understanding the woman involved was an important part of marriage.'

'I was wrong,' he said, surprised at how hard it was to admit.

'And what was it that led you to this revelation?' his brother asked.

'This morning, as I left the house, Maddie was entertaining a group of friends,' he said.

'An ordinary enough situation.'

'But she was doing it above stairs, in the nursery schoolroom. She appeared to be teaching some sort of class,' he said to Alex, still baffled.

'It might be trigonometry,' his brother said with a nod. 'Or calculus or probability. She has expressed interest in all of those to me, at one time or another.'

'What need does she have of them?' he said, feeling his nerves tighten at the thought of such instruction.

Alex shrugged. 'Perhaps she means to join the Navy.' When Evan did not laugh, he continued, 'I assume she needed the trigonometry for a better understanding of calculus. From what I understand, she was after a copy of Babbage's translation of Lacroix.'

'She said she had borrowed a book from Lady Byron,' Evan said. 'And that you introduced them.'

'Because they had similar interests,' Alex replied. 'Annabella Lovelace is an educated woman who married very unwisely. She could use a friend.'

'A friend like my Madeline?' he said, surprised.

'Your Madeline has an enquiring mind. She is very intelligent, as are many of the friends she is making. Since their husbands do not consider them thinking creatures, they bond with each other and share their knowledge. Didn't your wife mention to you that she desired to be a teacher or governess?'

'Rather than going home to her father? Yes. But I did not think she had any real inclination for the position.'

'Perhaps you are wrong,' he said with a shrug. 'Did she seem happy with what she was doing today?'

He stopped for a moment, considering the brilliant smile she had given him and comparing it with the placid happiness he was used to seeing. 'She seemed considerably happier than she is when embroidering,' he said with a frown.

'What reason does she have to do that?' Alex said, staring at him as if he should have an answer.

'All women stitch,' Evan replied automatically. 'Your mother stitched, as did mine.' Or so he'd thought. He had not known his mother, but there had been samplers in his nursery that were reported to have come from her.

'I wonder why?' Alex gave him a look again, as if he should understand the answer. 'My mother loathed needlework and made no bones about telling me so. And I must say I agree with her. Half of what is done in the name of the womanly arts is ornamental nonsense. I have never seen the point in monogramming handkerchiefs, since they are sorely abused and frequently lost.'

Without thinking, Evan touched the pocket where his wife's first gift to him resided. He had thought it good enough on the first night, only to see her take it back the next day and pick it apart to do again and again before she was satisfied with it. And then she had immediately started on another one. 'It took Maddie the better part of a week to make one for me.'

'As long as it would take you to work out her trigonometry problem,' Alex said, but there was no sense of judgement there, only a statement of fact.

And Alex, of course, could just as easily teach a class on the subject as his wife could. As he had seen before, the two of them had more in common than he ever would with Maddie. Once again, Evan pushed that thought to the back of his mind.

'Well, what am I to do with her?' he said hopelessly.

'Why do you feel the need to do anything?' his brother said with a bland expression.

'I am not sure,' he replied. But he was sure that there was something in his father's rules about the need to intervene when one's wife strayed outside the bounds of propriety. What was happening was not exactly improper, but neither was it ordinary.

But Alex had no such instructions and continued, 'It does not harm you in any way that she is teaching these classes, does it?'

'Of course not,' he said hurriedly. But why did he still feel this strange uneasiness when he thought of a room full of intelligent women with her standing at the front?

'Then I recommend you leave her be. It is not as if she is fomenting a rebellion or threatening the Crown. She is only studying mathematics.'

'Only mathematics,' he repeated, his stomach tightening at the thought. Then he admitted the truth. 'It would be easier if she liked any other subject. It is as if she is going to a place that I cannot follow.'

'Is there a reason to distrust her?' his brother asked.

'No. It is just that she is, by nature, a quiet creature.'

'How strange that you would think so,' Alex said. 'I would have called her gregarious, in the right circumstances.'

Perhaps that was the thing he feared. No matter how good they were together at night, it seemed that she had not yet found the right time to open up to him and to speak as freely as she did with his brother. 'She is still shy with me,' he admitted, though it pained him to do so.

'It has barely been two months,' Alex reminded him. 'You have a lifetime to change things.'

'I suppose so,' he agreed, trying not to think of his father and stepmother and the way the distance between them had grown greater with time.

'Do not worry about it now,' Alex said. 'Let us have another brandy and a round of cards. And when you get home, ask your wife about her day. I am sure she will explain all to your satisfaction.'

Chapter Fourteen

It had been the most delightful day she'd spent in a long time. Certainly the most intellectually stimulating. All the ladies she had invited to her mathematics salon had accepted, and they had eagerly copied her attempts at fresh enigmas, promising to return in a week with their solutions. Perhaps, next time, she could convince Annabella to join them, and prove to Evan that he had nothing to fear from the acquaintance.

But first she must prove to him that he had nothing to fear from the salons. She had assumed that Evan would be out of the house before her guests had arrived, and he would not see the outré way she was entertaining. It was not as if she needed to ask permission to use the room she chose.

But she had also seen the shocked expression on his face when he'd looked in on them, as if he could not decide whether to laugh or shout at her. In the end he had chosen aristocratic courtesy and left her to her friends. But she suspected, once he returned home, that he would be calling her 'Madeline' again and explaining that she had violated some rule of his father's that he had not yet told her.

At the moment she was in the sitting room with a vase of roses on the table in front of her, working on that afternoon's penitential watercolour. If she was honest, it looked no different than the painting she had done yesterday, other than the colour of the flowers, which had been blush pink and were yellow today.

Perhaps she could save time by sketching the same bouquet multiple times and changing the colours day to day. It probably did not matter, since no one was looking at the pictures, other than herself.

But for now she bit her lip and concentrated on laying a careful line of paint on the edge of a petal, trying to capture the way the colour faded from sunshine to cream.

'Painting, I see.'

At the sound of his voice behind her she flinched, and the resulting twitch of her hand dragged the wet brush across the paper, leaving a yellow drip through the middle of the flower.

'Blast.' She clasped her hand over her mouth, horrified at her involuntary response. She never cursed, not even in a whisper. She could hardly believe she had done so now, and in front of her husband.

'If you mean to gesture so wildly, perhaps you should put the brush down. You are getting paint in your hair.'

'Of course,' she said in a weak voice, setting the brush aside and turning to face him. 'I did not expect you,' she added, hoping that it was sufficient explanation for her behaviour.

'I am home early,' he agreed, but offered no explanation for it. Then he glanced over her shoulder at the watercolour in progress. 'Are you really so disappointed at a ruined painting?'

'It was an afternoon's work,' she said, which was really no answer at all.

'Where were you planning to hang it?' he asked.

She stared back at him, baffled. He had seen her painting before and always smiled in approval. But he had never expressed any real interest in what happened to the pictures. 'I really don't think my work is fit for public display.'

'Then you are painting to no purpose,' he said with a frown.

At this, she had no answer at all.

'Why do you do it?' he asked.

Her purpose had been to make him happy, and now it seemed he was not. But she was not about to admit something as humbling as that.

'Women are expected to keep busy,' she said, for that was as good an explanation as any.

'And how else do you plan to keep busy this week?' he asked. 'What will you be doing tomorrow at this time?'

Certainly not painting roses, if it was met with such an inquisition. 'Preparing food baskets for the poor,' she said, congratulating herself on how virtuous and wifely it sounded.

'And do you enjoy doing that?' Now his tone was faintly accusing.

'Yes?' she said softly, unable to hide the question in her voice as she aimed for the answer she thought he wanted to hear.

'You do not sound too sure of yourself,' he replied, still watching her closely.

Apparently, it was not the right answer, so she thought again, struggling for the words that would lift the clouds that were gathering on his face.

'It is an emotionally satisfying pursuit since one hopes to do good with one's life. If it is a question of salvation, I think the Papists require good works. But the Church of England...'

'I did not ask for a theological discussion,' he said, cutting her off short. 'I want to know if you personally enjoy the activity above others. Sewing, for instance. Is it better or worse than that?'

'Better,' she said, relieved to have an answer.

'And watercolouring. Where does that rank?'

'You wish me to rank my interests?' she said, thoroughly confused now.

He responded with a grim nod.

'Better than watercolour,' she said, 'which is even worse than stitching.'

'Even worse?' he repeated, as if she had confirmed something that he already knew.

'And pianoforte lessons are the worst of all,' she said, unable to stop herself. 'I have no talent for it and doubt I ever will.'

'Is that how you feel about traditional wifely activities?' he said in a clipped tone. 'You detest them?'

'I did not say I detested them,' she said hurriedly, wanting to quell his anger before it grew. 'They are simply things that women are required to do.'

'Required by whom?' he said, looking at her as if she had gone mad.

'By you,' she said, surprised to find herself becoming angry as well, and doing her best to stifle any sign of it. 'You told me to do as I pleased, but these are the things you seem to expect. I do them to please you.'

'Is there something you would prefer to do? Teach mathematics, perhaps?' The question was another accusation, and there was nothing she could do to avoid the answer.

'Yes,' she said, shocked at her own daring. She amended, 'Not teach, but…'

'Wasn't that what you were doing this morning?' he demanded.

'I was merely posing some problems that I had been working on in my spare time,' she said, searching for an explanation that did not sound so odd. 'They are mathematical puzzles, as one might find in the *Ladies' Diary* periodical. When I wasn't allowed to read it for myself…'

'You were not allowed…' he repeated.

'My father did not approve of my doing things that he did not think would impress my future husband. When he caught me reading the magazine, he slapped me and threw it in the fire.' And now it appeared that her father had been right all along. Evan was the last person who would understand her penchant for mathematics.

But, strangely, her declaration seemed to calm rather than anger him. He still looked grim, but he responded with a tight nod as if his suspicions had been confirmed. 'And what did you do then?'

'Nothing,' she replied. What was there to do but obey and avoid further punishment? Then she added cautiously, 'I sometimes amused myself by thinking up my own problems, but I did not bother to write them down.'

'That was your idea of amusement,' he said, his tone flat. 'Thinking about mathematics?'

She gave a small nod, then admitted, 'Some of the other women in London have similar interests. They read the *Diary*. And we happened to be talking about the latest enigma in the ladies' retiring room…'

'That is what you do there?' he said, surprised.

'Not always,' she said.

'And that is the reason you visit with Lady Byron,' he added.

'I do not visit her any more, because you disapprove,' she said, unable to keep the accusation from her reply.

He paused and took a deep breath, as if marshalling his emotions. Then he said, 'Why did you not explain any of this to me earlier?'

Because she had been afraid to. And now she could not decide if her fears were foolish or very real. 'I did not think you would like to hear it,' she said.

He closed his eyes and sighed, pausing again before speaking. 'You are right. As you have probably guessed, I do not enjoy mathematics and find calculation unusually difficult. But I like secrecy even less. And the thought that you have been pretending to be someone that you are not makes me very unhappy.'

'I am sorry,' she said quickly, wishing that she could undo the mess she seemed to have made.

'In the future, there must be no more lies, no more deception between us.'

'Of course not,' she said, relieved to see his smile return.

'You will not waste time doing things you do not enjoy, and I will not question your interests, even if I do not understand them. And there will be no slapping and no shouting. We will simply accept the fact that we are two different people and have different interests.'

'Could we?' she said, trying not to appear too eager at the thought.

'I don't see why not. My father and his second wife were quite different, and they managed just fine,' he replied, seemingly relieved to find an answer that fitted the rules he had been raised by.

Maddie was relieved as well. If his wife's different tastes had not bothered the previous Duke, then surely Evan could have no objection to hers. 'Thank you,' she said, and pushed herself away from the detested watercolour and into her husband's arms. 'Thank you, so very much.'

The next afternoon, at the club, Evan made sure his chair faced away from the clock, trying to ignore the passage of time and the feeling that his house was currently occupied by a stranger. For weeks, he had entertained himself with images of a happy bride wallowing in domestic bliss while he was away from home. But it appeared that her joyful domesticity had all been for show.

Yesterday, he had freed Maddie from the need to pretend, and the change in her had been instantaneous. First, she had called for a servant to drag the easel and paints to the attic. Then she had written a letter of dismissal to the music master. In the evening the mending basket had been relegated to the maids' room, and she had brought her books and papers to the sitting room, scratching away at them on a table in the corner of the room, rather than sitting devotedly at his side by the fire.

He had asked if she still wanted him to read and she'd assured him that he could if he wished, and that she was listening. But it baffled him that she could concentrate on two things at once.

And it appeared that he was not the only one bothered by the changes in his household. As the room filled, he was approached by a group of men who peppered him with questions about his wife's mathematical salon.

'Fallon! What is your wife getting up to during her morning calls?' the first one said.

'Getting up to?' he said, trying to ignore the unsettled feeling that he'd had when he'd seen the group of women in the nursery.

'Your wife has gathered half the women in town and is teaching them calculus.'

'Hardly half,' Evan said, forcing himself to respond as if it did not bother him as well. 'When I counted, there were not more than a dozen.'

'My wife has been doodling equations in her daybook,' said another man.

'And mine as well,' said a third.

'All this learning cannot be healthy,' said the first.

'It will overheat their brains,' an old earl said from his seat by the window. 'Women are not like us. They cannot deal with complicated processes.'

'And what need do they have for higher mathematics?' said another.

'As my wife explained it to me, they need it as much as many of us do,' Evan said, surprised to find himself leaping to her defence. 'And I see no sign that her studies have done my Madeline any harm.' Not as of yet, at least. 'She is still the mildest of creatures and exceptionally...' he struggled for a word that would mollify the men around him '...obedient.' She was very obedient. Except for such times when she was not. But that did nothing to support his argument. 'She gives me no trouble at all when we are at home together, and I see no reason to deprive her of her interests.' None other than his own comfort, at least.

'Then you have no intention of putting a stop to this?' the first man said.

'On the contrary, I mean to encourage it,' Evan replied, annoyed that they were still questioning him. 'If these women want to spend their time in study instead of gossip, it can only do them good.

If it proves too much for them, they will give up in a week or two.' And then, perhaps, things would go back to the way they were, when he was happily ignorant.

'That is true,' the second man said, brightening. 'I'd have never learned those things if not for a stern schoolmaster to rap my knuckles at each mistake. There is no way that they will carry on with it for just tea and biscuits.'

'Tea and biscuits with a duchess,' the old earl said in an ominous tone. 'Do not underestimate your wife's allure, Fallon.'

'Believe me, my lord, I do not,' Evan said, smiling and thinking of things that had nothing to do with mathematics. When she set her work aside at the end of the night, Maddie still invited him to her bed. In that respect, his wife had not changed at all.

Chapter Fifteen

The next morning Maddie attacked her breakfast with even more enthusiasm than usual, and smiled up the table at Evan as she heaped eggs onto her plate. He smiled back at her, a little confused, perhaps, but still happy. They'd made love last night, as they usually did, but it had been even better than usual. For the first time, she had felt that he knew her and accepted her as she was.

It still amazed her that she was married to such a wonderful man. He was staring down at the papers beside his plate with a look of intense concentration, and the furrows on his face only enhanced the clearness of his features.

'What are you looking at?' she asked, curious as to what work he'd deemed serious enough to bring to the table with him.

'The papers from your bank about the transfer of the trust,' he said without looking up.

'Oh.' In the excitement of Wednesday she had almost forgotten Mr Ramsey's plan, and the underhanded way he had forced her into making the decision.

'It is all percentages and compounded interest, and I cannot make head nor tail of it,' he said under his breath, then added, 'but I have no intention of signing until I understand.'

She reached out her hand for a moment to take them from him, then reminded herself that he had not offered to let her look. She must be patient and trust him, for she had promised her husband that she would not interfere in money matters again.

But that was before she had met Mr Ramsey and learned the influence he had over Evan in the handling of finances. There was something not right about the man. At the very least, he was overconfident in his position here. She supposed that was because he had been the old Duke's man of business as well. He had been here so long that deferring to Ramsey's judgement might as well have been one of Evan's notorious rules.

She continued to smile, her mind racing. She could not very well turn her dowry over to a stranger without having some idea of how he managed the funds already entrusted to him. How could she broach the subject to her husband, especially when she had no evidence other than a feeling? Since she had not spoken up earlier, he might think she was being feminine and foolish and did not know her own mind.

Perhaps, if she waited until Evan was gone from the house, she could sneak into the study for a quick peek. Parliament was in session today, so there would be no sudden reappearance by him, as there had been on Wednesday. He was not going to sign anything over breakfast. She still had some time to uncover the truth.

So she went back to her eggs and waited until they had both finished the meal and she had kissed Evan goodbye and wished him a good day. Then she crept to the study and sat down at the desk, sorting through the documents until she found the ones that described her trust.

The matter seemed straightforward enough, describing the transfer and combining of her accounts with his. But one thing surprised her. It appeared that all her money was to go into the household account, and not to a shared investment. Did they really need so much cash to be ready at hand?

There was only one way to tell. She went to the

shelf and brought down the ledgers, opening the books for the townhouse and the manor, leafing back through the months and searching for anything that seemed out of the ordinary.

What she found surprised her. There were multiple lines that seemed to be entered and subtracted twice, and a number of cheques made out to a Mr Ambersole, with no explanation as to who the man might be. Perhaps her husband had gambling debts. But he had made no mention of them to her, nor had he left the house in the evening without her in the weeks they had been married. The most recent of the strange expenses had been just days ago, when he had been at home most of the day.

And here were expenses for her that she knew she had not incurred. She had not been to a milliner since the first week. But if the ledger was to be believed, she had a taste for expensive hats and had bought several every week.

She settled into the chair and turned the pages back further, taking notes on a scrap of paper and trying to reconcile the final accounts with the money she suspected they had actually been spending. It was plain that there was a problem, and that it was no accident.

'Your Grace.' Ramsey was staring at her from the door of the study.

She had forgotten that her husband was not the only one who might be using the study. She hurriedly closed the ledger she had been reading and popped out of the chair, guilty that he had caught her in her husband's seat. But then she remembered that though he was a man, he was a servant and not a master over her and she held her ground and forced herself to meet his gaze without flinching.

'Mr Ramsey.'

'Is there something I might help you with?' he said in a cold voice.

'No, thank you. I am quite capable of reading these for myself,' she said, laying a hand on the ledger.

'And is that something that His Grace expects you to do?' He walked forward into the room and stood on the other side of the desk, reaching to take the book from her hand.

'That is between the Duke and myself,' she said. Her knees were shaking beneath her skirts but she took a deep breath and held her ground.

'Between the Duke and myself as well,' he said in an assured tone that made her skin crawl. 'It would be a shame if he were to find out from me that you have been snooping in places you have no right to be.'

He would tell on her, and then she would be in trouble. For a moment she heard her father's voice, warning her that disobedient girls deserved to be punished. She imagined the angry look on her husband's face and his hand raised to strike.

And then she told herself firmly that her father was not there, and never would be. He had been banned from the house and so had his punishments.

'You will not have to tell Evan,' she said, countering Ramsey in the only way she could. 'I will tell him myself when he returns home.' Then she did something she never would have dared before her marriage. She bluffed. 'I have already told him what I suspect.'

There was the barest flicker of alarm in the man's eyes at her threat. Then it was gone and he was calm and brazen again. 'Why would he believe you, over a man he has trusted since his father was alive?'

'Because I am his wife,' she said, too far gone in the lie to give it up. 'He knows I have his best interests at heart.'

'And he can also see that you are a woman and such things as the keeping of the accounts are far beyond you,' he replied, showing how little he knew about her. He reached for the books then, ready to take them away.

But she was quicker, sweeping them off the surface of the desk and onto the chair and out of his reach. A part of her was horrified by what she had done, and stood for a moment, waiting for the blow that was sure to follow such an act of defiance. But another part, a part growing larger by the minute, gave a cheer of victory as she recovered her nerve and sat down on them, grabbing the arms of the chair tight in her fists, lest he try to prise her from her seat.

Ramsey stared at her as if he could not quite believe what was happening. Then he took a step forward and said, 'Your Grace, you are behaving like a child.'

'Perhaps I am. But I am not going to move from this spot until Evan comes home.'

He inched closer and she realised that she had no idea what she would do if he was desperate enough to manhandle her out of the chair to get the ledgers back. Then a plan came to her.

'And if you touch me, I shall scream so loud that everyone in the house will come running,' she added, raising her voice as if preparing to do so.

In answer, Mrs Miller stuck her head in at the

door. 'Was there something that you wanted, Your Grace?' She looked back and forth between the two of them, puzzled. 'Tea, perhaps?'

'Mr Ramsey was just leaving,' Maddie said with a smug smile. Then she glanced at the clock. 'And I will take luncheon here at the desk, if that is all right.'

'As you wish,' the woman said, then gave Ramsey an expectant look.

He left the study with a final glare in her direction, and a few moments later she heard the front door slam. In his absence, she sat alone in silence, her heart racing over the recent confrontation and surprised that she had been able to manage it.

She trembled. And then the tears began.

When Evan arrived home later in the day, he was surprised to find his wife sitting in his study chair, a crumpled handkerchief on the desk and a grim expression on her face.

'Madeline?' he said, afraid of what was likely to come next.

She rose and pulled the ledgers off the seat of his chair, setting them on the desk.

'I thought I told you to stay out of my office,'

he said. 'And to keep your nose out of the account books.'

'I could not help it,' she said, not sounding the least bit sorry. 'You were talking about the transfer of my trust, and I was not sure I wished to do it.'

'You could have said something this morning,' he reminded her, frustrated. 'Or you could have never brought the matter up with Ramsey.'

'I did not,' she said. 'It was his idea all along. He has been pressuring me on the subject for weeks. And when he brought it to you, that morning at breakfast, he made it sound as if it was all my idea.'

'You said nothing to refute him,' he said, surprised. 'You could have come to me at any time.' Instead, she had kept it secret, as she had with so many other parts of her life. The thought hurt in a way he did not fully understand.

'He said you needed the money,' she said in a half whisper. 'I was afraid he might be right.'

'You do not trust me to take care of you,' he said as the pain in his heart grew sharper and more defined.

'I did not know what to think,' she admitted. Then her spine stiffened, and she opened the top ledger and tapped the page. 'But now I think I know the truth. Someone has to look into the accounts, for they are not accurate.'

'And that someone is John Ramsey,' he said, for she must know by now that he was an idiot when it came to numbers. 'He is the man I pay to do just that.'

'Ramsey is cheating you,' she insisted, pointing to the books with her fingernail. 'I see it here, and here. There are charges attributed to me that I never made. And you are continually writing cheques to a man named Ambersole.'

'Who?' he said, utterly confused.

'I suspect it is someone that Mr Ramsey made up to funnel money to himself,' she said with a look of triumph, tapping the book again.

'Don't be ridiculous,' he said, not wanting to believe it. 'He has been working for the estate since my father was the Duke.'

'Perhaps he has been cheating since then as well,' she said, frowning. 'We will have to go back through the books to be sure, but there are probably other entries that are false. Who knows how much money he has been keeping for himself?'

'*We* are going through the books?' he said, his hurt changing to anger.

'You, I mean. Of course,' she said, taking a step

away from the desk as if she could step back from her previous statement just as easily.

'And I am supposed to do this because you, a newcomer to the household, is convinced that a man who has held the position for years is not performing his duties?'

'It is not that he cannot,' she said. 'He is doing what he has done out of malice and self-interest because you are unfamiliar with the intricacies of running the estate.'

She had said the words he most feared to hear. 'Believe me, madam, I know it well enough.' At least he had managed so far. But he had done so with Ramsey's help.

'You know you do not,' she replied in a much gentler tone. 'You are very good at so many things. The best of men, truly. But when it comes to reading the account books, you have trouble.'

And that meant that he had failed in his duty to his father and to the Dukedom. He knew it was true, had always known so. But he had never expected that his own wife would put voice to his fears.

'It is not your position to tell me how to manage my affairs.'

'If the one who is closest to you in the world cannot tell you the truth, then who will?' she asked.

'Do not talk to me of truth, madam,' he said with a surprised laugh. 'You are truthful when it is a matter of my shortcomings, and happy to lie to me when it pertains to yours. You smile and say nothing when you are troubled, then sneak into this office the minute I am out of the house to take care of it yourself. In the future, when there is a problem, you are to come to me with it immediately, do you understand?'

'Yes,' she said, whispering again. She was white and shaking in the face of his temper, and he did not dare move, for fear she would flinch from him again, as she had on their first night of marriage. If she thought he would strike her, it was yet another sign that, no matter what she pretended, she did not trust him.

He could not stand the stricken look in her eyes, or the feeling that he had put it there. But neither was he able to cool his anger and claim that things were right between them. So he walked from the room and slammed the door behind him.

Chapter Sixteen

For the first time in weeks, Evan did not come to her bed.

Maddie wondered if it was by way of a punishment for her snooping in the books, or if he was still too angry to think of loving her. In the end, the reason did not matter, for the results were the same. She was cold and lonely and did not fall asleep until almost dawn.

When she greeted him the next morning at breakfast, he was as polite and courteous as ever, but made no mention of the previous day's argument. Perhaps he was waiting for her to apologise again for going behind his back to make the discoveries she had. She was more than willing to do so, if it convinced him to take action on the things she had found.

But, before she could do so, Mr Ramsey appeared

in the doorway, giving her a cold look before he took the place opposite her and turned to his supposed master for instructions.

Before he could speak, Evan did, giving more attention to the toast he was buttering than either one of them. 'I understand that there was a disagreement between you yesterday.' Then he looked up, favouring each of them with a direct and unwavering glance. 'It will not happen again. Do I make myself clear?'

There was really no way for either of them to answer this ducal command other than with a humble, 'Yes, Your Grace.'

'And the matter of the trust...' Ramsey added, showing more courage than Maddie could muster for herself.

'Will be dealt with by the time you get back from the country,' the Duke said before he could finish.

'I am being sent to the country?' he asked, surprised.

'I have an errand I wish you to run,' Evan said, tapping a letter that sat at the side of his plate. 'There is some question about the rents in the village that I wish settled immediately. The matter of the trust can be handled when you return in a few days.' Then he passed the letter he was holding to Ramsey and went back to his breakfast.

The man looked down at his plate, then back at the letter, as if trying to decide between the two of them. Then he pushed the food aside and tucked the letter into his coat pocket. 'I will be on my way, then.'

'Very good,' Evan replied.

With Ramsey gone, Maddie chewed furiously, her mind working over the problem. She had hoped that her husband would fire the man immediately upon seeing him. If not, there was the risk of him destroying the evidence of his crimes. But if Ramsey would not be in the house for several days, it was almost as good. It would give her time to persuade Evan to take action.

'Madeline.'

The word cut the silence and she looked up to see her husband staring at her with a neutral smile.

'Have you taken your necklace to the jeweller as I requested?'

She struggled with a mouthful of egg, her throat suddenly too tight to swallow. Then she answered, 'Not as yet.'

'Then go and get it, please. I will be on Bond

Street today, paying a visit to my tailor, and will take care of the matter myself.'

She froze, fork halfway to her mouth, unsure of what to do next. If she had remembered to take care of this herself, he would never have known that she had discovered the truth. But it was too late to wish for such a thing. She must show him the necklace and face the consequences of her actions.

As if he sensed something was wrong, he said, 'We will go to your room and get it together.'

She nodded and got up from her chair, leading the way up the stairs silently.

When they arrived at her room, she opened the dressing table drawer and retrieved the pieces of the damaged necklace, laying them out on the surface for him.

'What is this?' He stared down at it then glared at her, demanding an explanation. 'Is this how you treat my gift?'

'I did not mean to break it,' she said, taking a step back. Then she rallied her nerves and stepped forward again. 'But paste jewels are not as sturdy as real ones.'

'Paste?' Now his anger was tempered with confusion. 'What do you mean by that?'

'The stones are not real,' she said softly. 'I assumed you knew.'

'You assumed that I would give false stones to my Duchess, and represent them as real?' Now he was not just angry, he was outraged.

And the new spirit that had risen in her was angry as well. What she had felt or thought when he had given her the paste jewels did not bother him. Instead, he was thinking of how it would look to others and talking of his Duchess, the imaginary woman who was so important to him, and so different from who she was.

She sucked in a breath and answered, 'I did not know what to think.'

'And you didn't think to ask me?' This was softer, more hurt than angry.

'I was hurt,' she blurted out at last. 'So...'

'You said nothing,' he finished for her. His mouth twisted in a bitter smile. 'And I remained in ignorance of another important truth.'

'It is not as if I was lying to you,' she said, feeling weaker and smaller than she had in weeks.

'But you did lie to me. You told me the clasp was broken when I asked about the necklace,' he said, shaking his head in disappointment. 'If you had told me the truth from the start, I would have replaced the necklace.'

'Before someone else noticed,' she said.

'It would have embarrassed us both,' he agreed, not seeing the problem.

'Is that all that matters to you?' she said. 'Is the risk of seeming less to the world really so important?'

'It should matter to you as well,' he said.

'It did,' she said. 'I did not know until after dinner that the necklace was false, and I did not wear it again after that.' But it had mattered more to her than she had known. Looking at the necklace had made her feel as false as the diamonds were. Perhaps that was her problem more than it was his.

'I have told you before that there can be no more secrets between us,' he said. 'But after the day that has passed, I wonder if we can ever be together in truth and honesty.'

'I can change,' she said hurriedly. 'This is the last time I will give you trouble. I will be who you want me to be. I promise.'

'But you should not have to,' he said in a kind, sad voice. 'Any more than I should change my behaviour to please you.'

'I do not expect you to,' she insisted. But if he

did not change, at least a little, then how could she ever be good enough for him?

'We are two very different people, and we do not share the trust that we might have, had we met under different circumstances,' he said in an annoyingly reasonable voice.

'Of course,' she agreed. 'But that does not mean that we cannot grow together.' Every time they disagreed she felt a little less afraid of the consequences, and it became a little easier to tell him the truth.

'Or we can accept the fact that it will not happen,' he said, staring down at the necklace. 'This was never a love match, and there is no reason to pretend that it was.'

But she did not have to pretend. How could he not see that she loved him? She had never told him, of course. If she tried to do so now, he would just see it as one more lie of omission. And why would she tell him at all when it was clear that her feelings were not reciprocated?

He went on, ignoring her silence. 'I think it best that, after Ramsey returns to London, you begin your confinement in the country house.'

'My confinement,' she said, touching her stomach, which was still flat. 'That does not normally begin for some months.'

'They say the early months are even more risky,' he said with the authority of someone who knew nothing about pregnancy and childbirth.

'I will be careful,' she insisted. But at the idea of being banished to the country, all air seemed to have been sucked from the room. She groped for the dressing table chair and sat down suddenly, unable to support her own weight.

'I would rather be sure,' he said, as if her behaviour confirmed his plan.

'And what will you be doing?' she asked.

'I will remain here, in London.' His voice was cool and reasonable, as if he were speaking to an acquaintance about his plans. 'There is parliament to attend. And I would not want to disturb you.'

'You do not upset me in any way,' she said.

'Then perhaps it is you who upsets me,' he said with a sigh. 'You are not what I expected.'

'If it is the salons I am holding for the other ladies, I will stop them,' she said hurriedly, ignoring the creeping despair she felt at the thought.

'I would not expect that of you,' he assured her. 'You can spend time with whomever you like. It is possible that, once the succession is secured, we would both be happier if we found more suitable companionship.'

There was something in the way he said that word that made her think they were not talking about mathematics any more. They were not even talking about her female friends. They were talking about his. And if he thought she wished other male company...

'We cannot,' she insisted. 'We are married.'

'And we are about to have our first child,' he reminded her. 'It is not uncommon for couples to go their own way once they've had a son.'

Surely not couples who enjoyed themselves in the bedroom as they did.

'We will not know for months,' she countered. 'It might be a girl.' And what would his father have had to say about that?

'But should that child be the heir, your obligation to me will be fulfilled.'

It was not an obligation. Not for her, at least. But for him, having a son was just another one of his rules.

'Will one child be enough? More is customary,' she reminded him.

'We can see about that, when the time comes. But if I have an heir, there is no reason that you cannot be free to pursue whatever, or whoever, interests you.' Though he did not say so, that rule would apply to him as well.

'I am not currently preventing you from doing anything you want, am I?' she asked, feeling sick at the thought. Then she gave up her pride and added, 'If you want to take a mistress…'

'I certainly would not be speaking of that with you,' he snapped. 'That you would even say such a thing is indicative of the problems we are having. You seem to be incapable of keeping to the normal obligations of a wife and will not stop straying into areas that you have no business worrying about.'

'I will do better,' she insisted as she felt the new world she had found slipping away. 'I do not mean to displease you.'

'I know you do not,' he said with a disappointed smile that made her feel ten times worse.

'I don't know what you want from me,' she said as the flames of anger kindled amongst her misery. 'I have tried to do what you ask of me, and it does not make you happy.'

'I want you to be happy as well,' he said, though she had trouble believing it.

'When I am, you do not seem to be happy either,' she snapped. 'You do not like my friends. You do not like my hobbies. You treat me as an embarrassment. As a mistake that needs correcting.'

'And you lie to me because you cannot overcome the idea that I will hit you if you tell me the truth,' he said, rubbing his forehead.

'I never said...'

'You did not have to,' he replied sadly. 'That is why I think it would be better if we were to live apart.' He showed none of the fraught emotion she felt at the suggestion. 'You will have freedom to do as you want without fear of my input. And, in time, you will grow brave enough to stop hiding from the man you are with.'

The man she was with? He spoke as if there was no chance that the man might be him.

'Then perhaps it is for the best,' she said, rallying her nerves and striking back. 'It is clear that there is no pleasing you, unless I become an entirely different person.'

'You did not seem to be bothered by that when I first married you,' he said.

'Because I was lying,' she snapped. 'Everything I said and did was a lie, told to please my father, and then to please you. And now that I am telling the truth, I cannot even do that right. You cannot abide me.'

'That is not true,' he said in an unconvincing tone.

'It is. It is not the lying that bothers you. You cannot forgive me for telling you the truth about the diamonds and Ramsey.'

'It was not your place,' he said weakly.

'You seem to have a very good idea of what my place is,' she said with a grim smile. 'And I suppose that is another one of your father's rules. Keep your wife in her place.'

'It is a rule that society abides by,' he said, as if that should be reason enough.

'Well, I have had enough of rules, both society's and yours. You claim you do not want me to lie, but you were happier when I did. Even now, I do not know if you believe me about Ramsey. But if you did not mean to give me paste stones, they must have come from somewhere. Perhaps you should ask him.' She was panting now, overwhelmed by anger that she had never allowed herself to feel.

'I will,' he said. 'In my own good time.'

'And apparently I will not be here to see it,' she said. 'For you are casting me off to live in the country, while you stay here. You mean us to live apart, just as your father and stepmother, who could not stay in the same place.'

'They were happier that way,' he said. 'And if that

is what is necessary for us to live in harmony, we should do so as well.'

'Or we could try another way,' she said, pleading. 'Would it not be better to be two halves of a whole instead of two separate beings who make no effort to understand each other?'

'We have managed as two beings for most of our lives, and done just fine on our own,' he said, ignoring how miserable she had been before she'd met him. 'I suspect we will do well again, when we are not living under the same roof. Believe me, my dear, you will find that there is quite enough to do in the country that you will not even think of me.'

To believe that would be the biggest lie of all. If he could part from her so easily, he did not want to hear the truth: that she loved him more than life. But, before she could object again, he turned and left her alone.

Chapter Seventeen

After leaving his wife, Evan went to his study and locked the door behind him so that there could be no sudden interruption with entreaties for him to relent. He hoped Maddie was still too meek to question his decision, for he doubted that he could withstand her pleas if she did.

He was decided, and his father had always said, once a decision was made it was best not to second-guess oneself. Evan had brooded on this one all night, remaining in his room to do so. The only way he could think clearly when he was around her was to stay out of her arms and out of her bed. If that was not a sign of the shifting balance of power in their marriage, he did not know what it was.

When she had claimed to catch Ramsey in a lie, his first response had been shocked denial. That man had been hand-picked by his father and entrusted with everything but the keys to the manor. He had trusted Ramsey just as he had distrusted himself. If she was right, her discovery changed the whole course of his life. Until he could uncover the truth, he did not want her or Ramsey meddling with the accounts.

And now she had discovered false diamonds and, worse yet, she had hidden them from him. She had assumed that he was so poor he would pass glass off as precious stone, lying to society just as he'd lied to her.

He had expected the same honesty from her that he had given to her from the first moment of their marriage. But she had kept secrets from him, not just girlish nonsense but life-changing truths about his estate. In the night she was as uninhibited a lover as he could have hoped for. But in daylight she was still too afraid of him to speak openly, even when it was vital that she do so.

It was bad enough that he doubted her, but far worse that she made him doubt himself. If he gave her free run of his life, what else was she likely to discover that he had not noticed? And what was he to do about the things she had already found? Could it be true that the man he had been instructed to trust above all others had been stealing him blind?

The thought stuck in his craw, a constant irritant. The thefts, if there were any, must be recent. They never would have happened on his father's watch, since that man had been far too sharp to let such a thing pass.

And now there was the matter of the necklace. He pulled it from his pocket and dumped it onto the desk then rummaged in a drawer for a magnifying glass. He looked at the stones, one after another, wondering just what it was that he was expecting to see. She had noticed the difference almost immediately. But perhaps women had knowledge of jewels that men did not.

If so, it was one more area where his wife was better educated than he was. And again he felt the swell of panic, as if he had been thrown out to sea with nothing to cling to.

Then he noticed the scratches in some of the stones, probably ones that she had tested to establish their worth. Diamonds were not supposed to be fragile. These marks were a sign that it was not just a matter of a single false gem. He could probably take the necklace to a jeweller to see if any of the remaining stones were real. But to do so would require him to tell a stranger that he had been cheated.

And who had done that? The thief had to be in the house right now because he was sure that his father would have noticed had someone changed out diamonds for glass. But after his stepmother had died, the necklace had been all but forgotten in the safe in the study. Ramsey had the combination and could have switched the stones at any time and Evan would never have been any the wiser.

And none of his worrying got him any closer to solving the problems at hand. He must find someone to go through the books with a fine-tooth comb, inventory the entail and check that the jewels in the strongroom at Fallon Court were still real.

What he did not need was a wife picking through the rubble of the life he had once understood, withholding information from him, only to drop it without warning. He had to gain control again, to find what was wrong and make it right, and to show them both that he was the man he had always thought he was.

After her husband left her alone, Maddie stumbled across the room and climbed into her bed, pulling her knees to her chest and hugging her legs, closing her eyes tight against the truth.

Evan had cast her off.

At the thought, her breath came in short gasps of panic as she fought back the first sign of tears. She had known that he did not love her as she did him. But it had been enough to know that he wanted her, and that he was kinder to her than her father had been.

But apparently he had run out of patience with her. Or perhaps he had grown tired of her. Maybe that was the way of all men, to lose interest in their wives. But she had not thought it would happen so soon. And to say that they were too different? Of course they were different, that was the point of men and women.

She had lied to him, when he had told her not to. But they were such small lies, she'd never thought that they would amount to anything important. He was right that she feared him. But she feared everyone. She was trying to be better, but it was not something that was easy to change. And it was not going to get better if she ran from him now, back to the country, to hide in a house she had never seen before.

When she had the baby, would he want her again? The pregnancy had made him happy. Perhaps a son would make him want her again. Or a daughter would give him a reason to be with her.

But either possibility was months away. What would she do until then? How many watercolours did that equal, how many embroidered handkerchiefs and netted reticules, as she sat alone, far away from the new friends she had made and the man she loved?

Her hands were fisted, and the sudden awareness of the pain of her nails digging into her palms surprised her. She was angry.

It felt good.

Probably because what was happening to her was so unjust. She had tried to do everything he'd asked, and it had still gone wrong. He had called it all a lie and then rejected her when she'd been her true self. It made her wonder why she had even bothered to try and make him happy at all.

She stared at the wardrobe in disgust. At least now she could wear what she wanted and leave the fussy duchess gowns behind. She could wear plain muslin day and night if she cared to and devote her life to mathematics, minding her own trust and investing it as she pleased.

She could do anything she wanted. Evan had said it often enough, but he had really meant that she should do what he expected. When she actually had followed her own instincts, he had been either surprised or angry.

But his feelings no longer mattered. She would use her righteous anger to make her own way in the world. And that meant accepting her position and benefitting from it. She had a title. She had money. And, most importantly, she was married. She was no longer constrained by the restrictions her father had placed on her. She could truly do what she wanted.

There was a sudden, unexpected rush of excitement along with the anger. The idea that she might have some say in her own future was so novel that it overwhelmed her. What would she do with her freedom? If she could do whatever she wanted, what would it be?

She wanted to stay in London and be with Evan.

The idea was defiant, disobedient, and two months ago it was something she wouldn't have dared to think, much less do. It was the last thing her husband wanted, and the one thing he wouldn't expect of her. But unless he meant to pick her up and carry her there, he could not make her go to the country.

But what good would it do to stay?

She smiled. Anger was a powerful emotion. It

made her see things that fear did not. Evan might claim he didn't want her, but that was a lie. One night apart was hardly a sign of a permanent breach. It was more likely that he was sending her away to avoid the temptation of seeing her every day.

If she stayed nearby and did not allow him to forget her, it would not be long before he was begging her to come back to his bed. Once there, she would allow no more nonsense about living apart. They would be together for the rest of their lives.

She sat up and dried her eyes, a plan of conquest already forming in her mind. Even a few short days ago she would not have had the nerve to carry it out. She'd have believed the Duke of Fallon would never be influenced by a quiet country mouse. And she was certainly not the sort to stand up to men, especially not the ones in charge of her life.

But there must be a first time for everything.

When Evan came back to the bedrooms to dress for dinner, he was surprised to find that Maddie's room was empty, save for a maid who announced that Her Grace had 'gone out' and 'would not be home for dinner'.

Where could she have got to? They were entertaining Alex tonight, and he had assumed she would want to be there, since he had all but given her permission to cultivate the man as a favourite, if she so chose.

He doubted that she was headed for the manor house without so much as a goodbye. Ramsey was still there, and he did not think she was eager to see him again. Besides, when he looked in the wardrobe, her new dresses were still hanging there. She could not have run off without taking her clothing.

But when he asked the servants below, he was told that she had indeed called for a hired carriage and taken several trunks with her when she'd left. No one could tell him where she'd gone or how long she meant to be away.

When Alex arrived and heard the news, he looked at Evan with the bemused expression he had often worn when his little brother had done something particularly cloth-headed and was in need of rescue before the Duke found out. Then he said in an equally patient tone, 'What did you say to your wife?'

'Only that it would be best if we resided apart. We are quite different, you know. And there have been several instances lately where her behaviour has made my life more difficult, rather than easier.'

'Poor thing,' Alex said with a shake of his head.

'Her, or me?'

'You, you ninny. Now that she is coming into her own as a duchess, she does not need my sympathy. She will manage quite well, just as my mother did when she decided to leave your father.'

'That was her decision?' he said, surprised.

'I suppose you thought it was your father's, since he made a great show of controlling all elements in the house. But his own wife could not stand him.'

'They got along well enough,' he said with a feeling of unease at the memories that came back. He added, 'There was no love between the two of them, of course.' But then he had been told often enough that love was not necessary in the marriage of a peer.

'And then he announced that they were going to live apart on the day she decided not to leave London with him. It was an amazing coincidence,' Alex said with a smile.

'Well, it was my decision this time,' Evan replied, suddenly unsure that he had made the right one.

'I suppose she questioned your authority,' Alex said with a shake of his head.

'She did not even bother to do that. She just went ahead and did things without even asking,' he blurted out, embarrassed at how powerless it made him sound.

'How exciting for you,' Alex said, trying not to laugh.

'It was fine when it was just teaching mathematics. But she had taken to going through the account books. And she has come up with the outlandish idea that Ramsey has been embezzling.'

He had hoped his brother would laugh again, but instead, he sat up straight in his chair. 'She found signs of that?'

'I need your man of business to go over my accounts.' He held up a hand in warning. 'Discreetly, of course. I have packed Ramsey off to the country on an errand, so we have several days. And I am still not sure that anything is wrong.'

'If Maddie had doubts about the fellow, you have a problem,' Alex said with a frown. 'She is not likely to be mistaken over a matter of accounting.'

'I am aware of that,' Evan said softly. 'When I came home yesterday, she was behind my desk, sitting on the ledgers so he could not take them away from her.'

Alex snorted in amusement. 'Odd, but resourceful. And this was why you sent her away?'

'She also discovered that your mother's necklace

was paste. She thought I gave her glass,' he said indignantly.

'And what did she do about it?'

'Nothing,' he admitted.

'Probably because she did not want to embarrass you,' Alex replied with a nod. 'The girl is quite besotted with you, you know. But, given your feelings on love, I suspect she thought that glass was all she was worth to you.'

He had not thought of it in quite that way. With her timid nature, she would have seen it as a figurative slap in the face rather than a literal one. But he was surprised by the rest of the statement. 'Besotted?' he asked.

'You had not noticed the way she looks at you,' Alex said with a sigh.

'I thought…' *She was fond of you.* He shook his head. 'Never mind what I thought. You say she harbours feelings for me.'

'She is your wife. In normal households it is not considered unusual for women to love their husbands.'

He had not thought there was anything strange about their childhood, until today. 'She loves me,' he said, still surprised.

'Until today, at least,' his brother replied with a

smirk. 'If you think you had difficulties before, you have multiplied them now. But I will help you with one of the problems at least. I will send my man, Marks, round tomorrow, and if there is an issue with your accounts, he will find it.'

'Thank you,' Evan replied. 'And as far as the problem with Maddie goes...'

'You are on your own,' Alex finished for him. 'And, for God's sake, do not look to your father's rules to get you out of the mess you have made. He knew even less about what makes a happy marriage than you do.'

Chapter Eighteen

Before her anger had faded following her conversation with Evan, Maddie had hired a carriage and ordered the footmen to carry her old clothing down from the attic, where it had been stored when the new duchess gowns had arrived. Then she and her maid had transported the lot to the Clarendon Hotel, where she had a nice dinner and a good, if lonely, night's rest.

The next day she put on one of her favourite old gowns and found an estate agent to help her choose her new London home. The house she rented in St James's Square was not as opulent as the Duke's townhouse, but it was a sensible alternative to decamping for the country, as her husband had insisted she do. If she stayed in town, she would be able to keep the new life that she had been cultivating. She would also be near Evan, which was the most important thing of all. She would not allow herself to be tucked away in some manor house and forgotten.

Once settled, she sent cards to her friends, announcing her new direction and assuring them the weekly meetings of the Ladies' Mathematical Society that she had founded would continue until the end of the season, in her new home.

That should be all it would take for word to get round to her husband that she was defying him. In their brief marriage, he had heard about every other mistake she'd made in less than a day. She hoped that the gossips did not disappoint her now.

She had been in the house for less than a week when there was a knock on the front door, a short, angry rap of the knocker that carried all the way to the sitting room and made her start in panic. Before she could recover, a servant was hurrying to the doorway, one step ahead of her guest.

'Your Grace, you have a visitor.'

'Do not bother announcing me. I do not need to provide a card to see my own daughter.'

Her father. Here. Of course he would have heard the same gossip as her husband and would come to investigate. Her throat closed in fear at the thought of having to answer to him. Then she remembered that she was the Duchess of Fallon now, not simple Maddie Goddard.

'Father,' she said, turning to greet him with her most smooth duchess's voice.

'What have you done?' He took a step towards her, his posture rigid as if he was struggling to control his temper.

'What do you mean?' she said with an oblivious smile.

'It is all over town that you have left your husband after only a few months' marriage. How could you disgrace us in this manner?'

'Disgrace us?' she said, surprised to find that the anger she felt in response to this far outranked the fear. 'What does this have to do with you?'

'Your behaviour reflects on the family,' he said with some of the old bluster that had kept her in line for years. 'I demand that you go back to your husband immediately.'

This was where she would have to admit that her husband would not have her if she tried. When he realised that, he would slap her and call her a foolish girl. Then he would drag her by her hair back to the Duke or, worse yet, back to her old home. For a moment she could not breathe. Everything about her was frozen in place at the thought of the punishment to come.

Then, suddenly, the ice in her heart cracked and she said, 'No.' Her refusal surprised them both. But it had less to do with his current request than it did to the way she had been treated her entire life. It was a lifetime of rejection in one word. 'No,' she said again, savouring the feel of the word on her lips.

'You can't say no to me, girl,' her father spluttered, when he could find his voice. 'You had best remember your place. Or, by God…'

'Father, be quiet.' The words popped out of her mouth before she realised what she was saying. Perhaps it was Evan's fault for demanding that she tell the truth from now on. This was more honesty than she had shown to her father in decades.

'How dare you?' he said, his complexion turning florid in the way it did shortly before he lost control and struck her.

It was an excellent question. 'I dare because I am the Duchess of Fallon,' she said, squaring her shoulders and feeling the power of the title course through her in a way that would have made her husband proud. 'It is not so grand as being a duke, but it carries enough weight that I will have you thrown from the house if you cross me.'

He was still glaring at her, but he made no move and was, as she had requested, silent.

She went on. 'I can do much for you, as you hoped I would.'

'As the estranged wife of the Duke,' he said with a bitter smile.

'A duchess nonetheless,' she snapped, settling into her new role. 'And one who is willing to give you entrée into society, as long as you do not embarrass me.'

'You think I am an embarrassment?' he said, shocked.

'I know you are,' she replied, warming to a subject that she had long wished to discuss. 'You talk more than you listen, even when the men around you deserve your respect and your silence. And when I lived with you, you took pleasure in terrorising my mother and myself.' Just the memory of it made the blood pound in her ears, but she went on. 'I will not stand for it any more. If I ever hear of you laying a hand on Mother again, I will see you cut from society without another thought and leave you worse off than you were before.'

'You would not dare,' he said, and she could see by the twitch in his hand that he longed to use it against her.

'Strike me and see,' she said, and waited a full thirty seconds before speaking again.

For a moment he considered it, half raising his hand before letting it fall to his side again.

She smiled. 'You do not control me any longer.'

'I will go to your husband with your disobedience,' he said in a grumble with no real power behind it.

'If he wanted to quell my behaviour, I would not be here,' she said with a smile that surprised herself. 'I am my own woman now and will do as I please. And I do not wish to talk to you any longer today. If we meet in public, I will acknowledge you, as long as you leave me in peace. If not, I will do my best to ruin you.'

'This is not the end,' he said, standing up.

'Yes, it is.' Now she could not stop smiling, and the feeling of freedom as she watched him depart was undeniable. Then she went back to the enigma she had been writing and thought no more about him.

When next he went to the club, Evan learned that his wife was still in London. As soon as he'd taken his seat, several men had come to him to announce her new address, and their wives' plans to continue their mathematical instruction at the new location.

To the first, he had responded with frigid silence, refusing to give them the satisfaction of knowing that they had answered a question he had been afraid to ask. Then he told them that their wives' plans were none of his affair. The fact that Maddie meant to continue her mathematical society was the best news to come of their estrangement. How much trouble could she get into, if all she meant to do was gather with other ladies?

In her absence he had problems of his own to deal with. When he came home from the club, it was to discover that Ramsey had returned from his trip to the country and was in his study, searching for the ledger books, which were now under lock and key at the bank. He was probably hoping to make reparative changes that would hide his embezzlement.

'Your Grace?' he said in a subservient tone that now seemed false and ingratiating.

'Looking for something, Ramsey?' Evan said, taking his seat behind the desk and staring at the man until the silence between them grew long and awkward.

'I had entries to make in the accounts,' he said, his gaze darting helplessly around him.

'I imagine you did,' Evan replied. 'There is much you need to hide, now that I know what to look for. Mr Ambersole, for example.'

'I am not sure...' the man said, trying to hide his panic in false confusion.

'He is a man to whom I am paying a regular salary, yet I have never met nor heard of him,' Evan reminded him.

'The books were fine,' Ramsey insisted. 'Until the Duchess began working on them.'

'It is Madeline's fault now, is it?' Evan said in a warning tone.

'You had no complaints before,' Ramsey reminded him.

'Because I trusted you, as my father did.' And he had been a fool. 'But now I have audited the books and have found your embezzlement.'

'Because she told you to.' Ramsey's eyes narrowed with an unjustified spite.

'Be careful of your words,' Evan said. 'You have feathered your nest with my money, believing that your relationship with my father put you above reproach.'

'It has not mattered to you until now,' he said with a shrug. 'Perhaps if you had the ability to read the books, as you should have...'

'I do not need to be able to read the ledger. I need a person in your position who can be trusted to read it for me,' he said, cutting off the man's excuses. 'Since it is clear that you are not that person, you are being sacked without reference. Men have been hanged for less, but for the sake of my reputation I am willing to spare you a trip to Newgate, if I receive a substantial cheque from Mr Ambersole, by way of reparation.'

Ramsey said nothing, but a look of relief replaced the smug confidence that he'd shown a few moments ago.

'And of course, I want to know what happened to the diamonds,' Evan added.

'What?' Ramsey said, clearly shocked. He took a moment to gather his wits and replied, 'For the first, there is nothing I can do but apologise and write the cheque. We can go to my bank and clean out the account if that is what it takes to satisfy you. But in the matter of diamonds, I can tell you nothing. I do not even know what stones you are talking about and will swear on anything you might believe that I cannot help you.'

Evan stared at him for a moment, waiting for a sign that he was being lied to yet again. But there was a frantic sincerity in Ramsey's manner that was unlike his smooth demeanour of a few moments ago. It appeared that, whatever had happened to the necklace, he'd had no part in it.

Later, when he had returned alone from Ramsey's bank, Evan sat at his desk, unsure of what to do next. Underneath the numb exhaustion he felt after dealing with the embezzler was the desire to laugh out loud. He had assumed that there was something about his own behaviour that caused the continual shortage of funds. But it had been Ramsey all along.

It was apparent that he had been stealing from Evan for some time. To save his own skin, he'd written a cheque almost as large as the one Evan had received as Alex's wedding gift. It was fortunate that the man had not taken control of Maddie's trust, or the damage might have been even more severe.

He would need a new man of business, someone honest to read the books to him and show him where the money had gone and how to repair the damage done to the Fallon accounts. But once that was done there might be no more problems with the finances.

In any case, the things his father had taught him about trust in staff and good stewardship had been largely useless. He might never have put faith in

Ramsey if it hadn't been for his father's endorsement. And it was clear he lacked the skill to manage money matters himself. If it had not been for Maddie's interference...

And what was he to do about her? He had thought that if he sent her away, his life would go back to the uncomplicated routine he had enjoyed before they'd married. But it seemed not. His meek little wife refused to retreat and intended to remain in London, though not in his house, making them the talk of the season.

What would his father, that font of all wisdom, have done in a similar situation?

That answer was clear enough. He would tell the world that the separation was all his doing, pretend to be glad of it and ignore the talk. And then go on keeping a careful distance from his wife for the rest of their lives.

It seemed that, despite what he had hoped for, he was to have his father's marriage after all.

Chapter Nineteen

That night was to be Evan's first outing as a free man.

Not quite free, he supposed. He was promised to go to a ball thrown by the Duchess of Andover and did not want to beg off and spend the evening as he wished, with a book in the library. As he had always known, appearances were everything and, with rumours of his break with Maddie already circulating, he did not want to give the *ton* the impression that the parting had been done in passion.

It was best to let the world see things exactly as they were. Theirs was a sensible separation of two people who had nothing in common other than the union society had forced on them.

It felt wrong to be alone, as if he was stepping into public totally naked and without defence. The feeling was ridiculous. Until recently, he had never had a wife and had moved easily in society. How could he miss her so much after less than a week apart?

He should focus on the advantages of being alone. He just had to remember what they were. He would not miss her meddling in his money. Of course, that meant that if he chose the wrong replacement for Ramsey, there would be no one to tell him so and he would continue to blunder on as he had, the errors growing bigger and bigger until they engulfed him. But that was a matter for another time.

Tonight, the most important decision he needed to make was who he would waltz with. Or perhaps it was better not to waltz at all. Slow, intimate dancing only reminded him of what he had decided to deny himself, at least until after the child was born.

When he had sent Maddie away, he had not been thinking of prolonged celibacy. It was certainly possible for a man to have his needs met with discretion. But the idea was strangely distasteful. There was nothing in his father's rules about being a faithful husband, but now he could not seem to be comfortably unfaithful.

The whole train of thought was nonsense. It was not as if his wife had died. She had not even left the city. He could visit her if he wished, just for a night.

She would take him in, he was sure. Alex had said she loved him. If that was true, she would be missing him as much as he missed her. Not that he missed her, actually. But he definitely wanted her.

Perhaps she was pining for him right now, wishing that he would come to her. And he would do so, in a week or two. He must wait until some time had passed, so he did not seem too dependent.

But tonight he was alone, and must pretend to be happy about it. When he arrived in the ballroom, heads turned, as he'd expected they would, with an interest quite different than he had felt when he was unmarried. Then, it had generally been the mothers of unmarried females who'd noticed him, like lions on the veld spotting an antelope.

Now, everyone stared at him because he offered something even more delicious than marriage: gossip. They stared and then turned back to whisper to each other, remarking on his presence, her absence, and tut-tutting over the sudden change in their equally sudden marriage.

'Evan.' Alex was there, greeting him with a nod, and a smile that was a little too broad to suit the occasion.

'Alex,' he said, smiling back with what he hoped was his premarital joie de vivre.

'I did not expect to see you here,' his brother said, still smiling. 'No one did.'

'My wife may be gone from my side, but I see no reason to become a recluse,' he responded with a shrug.

'Neither does she.' Alex stepped aside to give him a clear view of a crowd of men on the other side of the room.

Evan heard the laugh before he saw her, the sound dancing along his nerves and raising the fire in his blood before he knew how to respond. He must be imagining it. It could not be Maddie. She rarely laughed in public. She was circumspect when out amongst the *ton*, quiet and reserved.

What he had just heard sounded like the laugh she gave when they were alone together, the free, easy sound that made him laugh in response.

It made him wonder who she was with and why she was so amused. Then the crowd parted, and he saw her.

Pregnancy suited her. It would be months before there was any real evidence of the child growing inside her, but her colouring had changed from the wan misery of those first days to a rosy pink. Her breasts filled her gown in a way they had not before.

Or perhaps it was simply that she was wearing a

different style. The dress she wore was an embroidered white muslin that clung to her curves and let her charms shine through in a way that her other gowns had not. When he had last escorted her to a ball, there had been no question that she was a duchess. She had been dressed like one. But tonight she was something even more than that, beautiful, desirable and with a knowledgeable air that had nothing to do with calculus.

Others were noticing it as well. Men were crowded around her, both single and married, hanging on her every word. And before he knew what he was doing, he was walking towards her, fists balled and ready to argue.

But it was like meeting a stranger. Instead of giving him the soft, soothing smile she had worn as she presided at his table, she beamed at him, glittering bright and artificial as the necklace he had given her. 'Fallon.' Her tone was perfectly tuned, loud enough to call all attention to them without appearing to shout. If he had wanted this to be an amicable parting, he could not fault her manners. They were impeccable.

'Madam,' he said, frigid. 'You are supposed to be in the country.'

'I decided not to go,' she replied with a smile he

had never seen before. 'It is too early for a confinement, don't you think? I would much rather enjoy the rest of the season and retire once the last parties are over.'

'I will be going to the country when the season ends,' he said, reminding her of their plans to remain apart.

'There is always Bath. Or I hear that Bristol is nice.' She tipped her head to the side as if considering.

Another fraud. He had never seen her take that pose before, calling attention to the kissable line where chin met throat.

Then she spoke again. 'Or I could simply go to the country with you. I have not seen it as of yet, but Alex assures me that the house is very large for two people.'

Even larger for one. He avoided it because it was too lonely. Until recently, he had been looking forward to sharing it with her.

'I do not think that is wise.'

'Then perhaps I shall stay in London,' she said. 'It is unfashionable in the off-season, but there is still much to do here.'

'Or you could return to your parents,' he suggested, setting his jaw.

Instead of cringing at the thought, she laughed as if he had made a joke. 'That is Lady Byron's plan after her child is born. I did not think you wanted me to emulate her in any way.'

'You know that is not what I meant,' he said through clenched teeth.

'Of course, you have also told me on multiple occasions that I can do whatever I want,' she said, touching a finger to her chin as if showing him where to nibble. 'And the last thing I want in the world is to climb back under my father's thumb. I have decided to obey you in that, at least.'

'At least,' he repeated, temper boiling.

'I have taken a house in St James's Square. Not the most fashionable neighbourhood, but I can well afford it. And I mean to make the destination popular.'

Did she mean by night or by day? She was certainly not acting like a woman content with teaching mathematics to her coterie of dissatisfied wives. If that was all she wanted, then she should act like a schoolteacher and not a flirt.

'I forbid it,' he said, surprised to see the rebellious light in her eyes.

'After sending me away, you lost the right to direct my behaviour,' she said with a shrug.

'You are still my wife,' he reminded her through clenched teeth.

'And we both know how little that is worth to you,' she said with a pitying shake of her head. 'Now, if you will excuse me, the dancing is beginning, and my card is full.' Then she reached out and took the arm of the nearest gentleman and swept past Evan onto the floor and into a waltz.

Maddie stared into the eyes of her dance partner, smiling brightly. Talking to Evan had been the most frightening thing she had ever done. Even now, she fought the desire to turn back to him, to apologise and go meekly to the country where he wanted her to be.

But to give in so easily was to lose all.

Right now, she was waltzing, the most provocative of dances to a jealous husband. Was he that? she wondered. It certainly appeared so, but she still did not have the confidence to believe it. She was wearing one of her favourite gowns instead of the kind he had wanted her to wear. It was one more form of rebellion to experiment with and she decided she enjoyed it.

She was sure that he had noticed the difference, but the look in his eyes had been appraisal not disapproval. And the other men at the ball had commented favourably on the difference. Was it just the absence of a husband that drew them to her side, or was she really looking her best tonight?

She was surprised to find she did not care. She felt her best and that was the important thing. She felt desirable and not like the little country mouse that her husband had once accused her of being.

Her partner spun her again, and this time she laughed out loud.

The gentleman smiled back at her, dazzled.

She didn't want him to be dazzled. She wanted Evan to be dazzled. But it seemed she had made him angry again, just as she always did.

Then the dance was over and her partner escorted her back to a chair along the wall, offering lemonade or a plate of dainties from the buffet. She thanked him with a fluttering of her fan, wondering if this was what having a season might have been like. She had missed the joy of that because of her father's iron-clad plans for her future.

Of course, there had been gains as well. The nights in Evan's arms had been better than wasting time flirting at Almack's. She smiled in his direction and raised her glass of lemonade in a salute to him, taking a polite sip.

He stared back at her, simmering with rage, shrugging off the comments of Alex, who stood next to him. Then he turned away.

Alex strode across the room to her, dismissing the men who hovered at her side with a ducal shake of his head. 'What you are doing to him is most unfair.'

'What I am doing to him?' she said with a surprised expression. 'He cast me off, you know. He thinks I am lying, interfering and troublesome. He says we have nothing in common but the child and thinks that I will conveniently disappear until it is born and he knows whether he need visit me again.'

'I did not say he is not being a fool,' the other Duke admitted. 'But men are fools when they are in love and there is nothing that can be done about that.'

'Love?' she said, shocked.

'You did not know?' he said, surprised. 'It is quite obvious to me, but I have known him most of my life. He is in love with you and doesn't know what to do about it.'

'That is simple enough. He should take me back,' she said, staring at the doorway as if she could will him to return.

'If it were simple, he would never have parted

from you,' Alex said. 'You challenge what he has always believed about his life. He was told that being Duke was all that mattered. And now it is not enough for him.'

'And I suppose that I am that thing that he lacks,' she said with a bitter smile. 'Hasn't he told you that one woman is like the next?'

'He may have said something as idiotic as that,' Alex admitted with a smile.

'Then surely he does not need me.'

'On the contrary, he needs you like life itself and will realise it directly.'

'If all I have to do is wait for him to change his mind, then you might as well tell me I have failed. He is adamant that we stay apart.'

'Just as he was convinced that his father was wise in all things. You are teaching him otherwise and it is a very difficult lesson, more difficult even than calculus would be for him. And now that he knows we are speaking, he is likely to be an even bigger fool than before.'

'Whyever for?' she said with another laugh.

'Because he thinks that I am trying to gain advantage in his absence, just as the rest of the men in the room are. I have known him since he was ten and have never seen him jealous before. Probably because he has always had more than the men around him and was able to maintain it effortlessly by right of birth. There was no chance that his title would run off and leave him for another man.'

'And neither will I.' She glanced quickly around the room and the men she had been flirting with. 'I am not interested in them. Or in you either,' she added, hoping that he was not too insulted.

'That is good to know,' he said with a kind smile. 'It would make things much more difficult for him if you were faithless. As it is, he fears that, now you are close to him, you see only his weaknesses, and not his strengths.'

'He is not perfect,' she said with a shake of her head. 'But then, none of us are.'

'That is an excellent opinion to have,' Alex agreed. 'And when he arrives at it, I expect he will come knocking on your door to tell you so. But until that time, try not to be too hard on the fellow.'

'I will take your words under advisement,' she said, though she found it hard to believe they were true. Then her next dance partner came to claim her and she did her best to forget all about them.

Chapter Twenty

Evan left the ball early and went to a gambling hall. There, he drank too much and lost too much as well. His intent was to stay until dawn, to sink himself in vice. He was free to do so, now that there was no one waiting for him at home. Or perhaps he wanted it because there was no one waiting for him at home. He was no longer sure.

But despite, or perhaps because of the fact, he retired at a little after two, staggering home to the empty bed in his empty house, falling into a fitful sleep.

He dreamt about *her*. Not as she was when she was in his house. He imagined her as she had been at the ball, gowned in white and sparkling like the diamonds he should have given her.

He woke and tossed in his bed, reaching for the empty space where she should be. Where she might have been if he hadn't sent her away. Had she found someone to keep her company on this night? Was it Alex?

For a moment he felt something very like panic at the thought. Would she really forget him so completely? When she had lived with him, he'd found her to be too interested in his business. Now, he feared that she did not think of him at all.

He did not want to believe she'd be unfaithful, and it had been idiotic to give her his blessing. His brother had gone to her as soon as she had stopped dancing and they had talked for almost fifteen minutes. He had stood in the shadow of the doorway, staring at them the whole time.

It had been an eternity for him, standing on the other side of the room and pretending that it did not matter. And there had been that moment when she had glanced across to him and raised her glass in a toast, smiling as if she knew something that he did not.

Of course, she had already proved on multiple occasions that she knew more than he did. But he'd had no idea that a woman who had been an innocent a few months ago could wield her newly found seductive prowess like a weapon against the man who had taught her.

He was not her only victim. Half the men at the ball had gone weak in the knees when she'd smiled, crowding around her for a moment's attention. And he, fool that he was, had given her permission to seek attention elsewhere, if she wished.

After that thought there was no way sleep would come. He thrashed his way out of bed and walked to the connecting door that separated him from her room.

The fire was not lit, but it was better in darkness for the room still smelled faintly of her cologne and, with his eyes closed, he could imagine that she was still there, in the bed beside him. In the past, he had not bothered to remain with her after they'd made love, not realising how precious the time was. This night, he stayed until dawn, unsatisfied and alone.

The next morning, he crept back to his own room before his valet could find him hiding in hers. Once he was shaved and dressed, he noticed the jewellery case from the diamonds, still sitting on his dresser. The name of the jeweller that had made it was printed in gold on the satin lining. That man would know better than anyone else the condition of the current stones. He could handle the restoration discreetly. Then perhaps Evan could give it as a peace offering to his wife, on the birth of their first child.

He went down to the study to get the broken necklace, then called for the carriage to be brought round to take him to Bond Street.

When he arrived at the shop, the jeweller dropped his loupe in surprise and came out from behind the counter, offering a deep bow. 'What can I do for you today, Your Grace? A purchase for your lady wife, perhaps? Or for someone else?' Apparently, word of their separation had reached the merchant class, and the fellow hoped for profit from both sides of the rift.

'No,' he said, embarrassed at the thought. 'I was hoping for some information on a necklace you have already sold to the family. It is a matter of some discretion.'

The man laid a finger across his lips and nodded. 'No word shall ever pass from me.'

'Very good,' he replied, then fished the necklace out of his pocket and laid it on the glass-topped counter. 'I need to know how many of the stones in this necklace are real, and how many have been replaced by paste.'

The jeweller smiled and nodded. 'That is indeed my work, and it is easy to tell, without even looking. All the stones are false, just as they were when I sold it to your father.'

For a moment he was not sure of what he had just heard. 'They were never real?' he said, hoping that the shock in his voice was not too evident.

'That is what he requested, and what I made for him,' the jeweller said with a nod. 'He wanted a wedding gift for his new wife, but was not interested in real stones. He requested high-quality paste, something that could not be told from real if worn in candlelight. And, as you can see, the necklace is quite spectacular. Or at least it was until someone destroyed it,' the man said with a frown. 'If you wish me to replace the missing stones…'

'No,' he said quickly, snatching the offending thing back and putting it in his pocket again. 'That will not be necessary.'

'Then perhaps a parure for your new duchess. I have some fine amethysts in the safe right now, set in gold. If they do not please you, I could make something more like the necklace in your pocket.'

He was suggesting that Evan buy false stones and pass them off as real, just as his father had. Where was the truth and honour in that?

'No! When I am ready to buy something, I want

nothing but the best. But not now. Not today.' Today, he was in no mood to shop for anyone.

'As you wish,' the jeweller said with a disappointed nod.

He walked back out of the store, and down the street, the necklace heavy as lead in his pocket. Were the rest of the Fallon jewels false as well? Perhaps not, for his father had inherited them rather than buying them. The jeweller had said nothing about other requests. But then, Evan had not asked him. If his father had made a habit of lying, he did not want to know.

He stopped on the pavement as the idea hit him like a blow to the stomach. His father, a man obsessed with honour and honesty, had requested this travesty as the first and only gift he had given Alex's mother.

What had his father felt for his second wife? There had been no trace of love in the union on either side. He had always assumed that the marriage had begun with some degree of affection, or at least a mutual respect. But if even the wedding gift had been a sham, what did this cruel trick say of his father's character?

And what did it say that his father had held Ramsey up as an example of a loyal and competent servant? He had wasted years assuming that his money troubles were his own fault due to his general incompetence with numbers. But his real weakness had been the blame he'd placed on himself and his slavish devotion to instructions that his own teacher had not bothered to follow.

It had taken someone with fresh, innocent eyes to see the errors in his philosophy, as she'd had that first day, with the books.

For a moment, the world seemed to shake beneath him, or perhaps it was just the crowd on the street bumping against him as he blocked their way. He had to move.

He began walking with no destination in mind other than to get away from where he was. Without thinking, he picked up his pace, outstripping the crowd. Then he went faster still, until he was running down Bond Street. He was sweating and panting with the effort, but he did not stop. His coat flapped as he ran and the necklace in his pocket banged against him like a heartbeat, urging him forward. In his mind, a single word rang over and over with the same rhythm.

Wrong.

His slavish devotion to his father's teachings.

Wrong.

The man himself?

Wrong.

The careful world he'd built for himself. The spotless family image. His trust in Ramsey.

All wrong.

People were staring at him, shouting and muttering as he pushed past them without apology, trying to outrun the truth. He raced breakneck for the end of the block. Behind him, he heard his carriage, the driver shouting into traffic to make way as he tried to keep up with the master.

Evan reached the corner, still not sure where he was going, and darted across the street, dodging carriages and people, making it another two blocks before his wind gave out. He stopped, doubled over, gasping and sweating as he tried to think.

Until today, his father had been the shining example of the kind of man he'd wanted to be, forthright, intelligent and wielding the power he'd been given with iron control. But he'd ignored the man's flaws, the coldness, the casual dismissal of those he could not use and the streak of petty cruelty with which he'd treated his wife.

What must Maddie have thought of him, with his rigid expectations and his obsession with what the world thought of her behaviour? He had expected her to fit into his life like a piece into a puzzle and had been ready to sand down any lumps and bumps in her character that might stand in the way of his image of perfection. He'd believed all women were the same and had been annoyed when she had not fitted into his life without effort.

He had not appreciated that she was perfect just as she was. He certainly had not considered that he might be the one who needed to adjust to her.

She had seen that changes needed to be made and had done her best to make him a better man. She had improved his life for him, and he'd complained all the while. And she'd been willing to forgive him, over and over, for the things he'd done to her. And wasn't that what one really wanted in a wife?

He was grinning now, tired but aware of his goal. St James's Square was still over a mile away, but he had homed in on it like a pigeon, running towards it before he even knew the reason. And now his carriage had caught up to him, a worried footman hopping down from his perch to help the master, who was clearly running mad.

'I am fine,' he said, shaking off his servant's assisting hand. 'Better than fine,' he added with a reassuring laugh. 'And I will be better still if any of you can tell me the direction of my wife. St James's Square. I do not know the number.'

Then he climbed into the carriage and set out to get his future back.

Chapter Twenty-One

Maddie looked out over the faces of her friends, gratified that, at this difficult time in her life, she was not alone. She was having the first meeting of the Ladies' Mathematical Society in what she feared might be their permanent new home, the cramped sitting room of her little house on the square.

She found the room to be rather dreary, compared to the spacious and comfortable townhouse of the Duke of Fallon. But she had no idea when she might be allowed back there, especially after goading Evan last night at the ball.

It was kind of Alex to say that her husband was in love with her, but as yet she'd seen no sign of it. He had not declared himself last night, nor had he given any hint that he might be open to further communication with her. In lieu of that, she must keep accepting invitations and bump into him when she could, like two marbles rolling around in a jar.

The mathematical probability of seeing him was an interesting enigma in its own right, given the number of people in London and the pool of common acquaintances. She had devoted far too much time to the problem last night, when she'd been trying to sleep. But she did not want to think of it at the moment. It might lead to frustrated tears, which would seem strange to the group gathered to try their hands at her latest puzzle.

The crowd today was even larger than the one she had entertained in the schoolroom, and included a few hopeful young gentlemen, who had probably not expected that they would be sitting through a lesson in calculus. If she wanted to give the impression that she did not mind her husband's displeasure, she could not send those fellows away. But it was not in her nature to flirt, especially not outside the ballroom, where dancing required a certain degree of conversation.

So she welcomed the confused gentlemen politely, offered them tea and biscuits and then took her place at the front of the room, where a chalkboard had been erected, to begin her lecture.

As she did so, there was a knock on the door and

the sounds of bustle in the entrance hall as a late-comer arrived.

She paused in her speech to give the lady time, only to be surprised by the familiar masculine voice that was speaking with her maid.

'Are you expected?' the girl asked him, showing far more nerve than a smart Fallon servant should have.

'I seriously doubt it. But do not bother to announce me. Treat me as just another of her admirers.' Then he appeared in the doorway, standing framed there for a moment with the same confused expression he had worn when he'd interrupted her last class in the nursery.

There was an audible gasp as some of the more gossipy ladies realised his identity, and a sigh of disappointment from at least one of the men.

Then Evan said, 'Do not mind me. I seem to be late.' He waved off the greetings of the ladies and the looks of terror on the faces of the men he had caught courting his wife and took a place at the back of the room, leaning against the mantel of the fireplace. Once comfortable, he added, 'Please, continue with your lecture.'

She went back to the lesson. It was difficult to concentrate with him there. As he ever was, he was a distraction. If possible, even more distracting than usual. In the stolen glances she took of him when she was not writing on the board, she had to wonder if he was well. His usually immaculate day clothes were dishevelled. The knot of his cravat was lopsided, as if it had been loosened and hastily retied. His face was flushed from exertion, the waves of his hair damp against his forehead. He reached into his pocket to retrieve one of her badly embroidered handkerchiefs to mop his brow.

Whatever he had been doing, he was smiling as if he'd enjoyed it. It reminded her of how he'd looked after they'd made love. The thought made her lose her train of thought so completely that she was silent for almost a minute, fumbling with her notes to hide her confusion.

Then she found her place again, and went back to explaining differential equations. Some of the women in the room understood and others questioned her on her findings, so she answered in detail, leaving several of her guests baffled and scribbling quickly in notebooks while asking for more clarification.

Through it all, her husband stood patient and smiling, though she suspected that he did not understand a word of what she was saying. But he made no move to interrupt, letting her go on for almost an hour. When she had finished speaking, there were more questions and some polite applause, and slowly the group dispersed, leaving him standing alone at the back of the room until she decided to acknowledge him.

After she had shown the last lady to the door, she returned to find that he had taken a seat on the sofa, his legs stretched out in front of him, as comfortable as if he owned the room.

For a moment she wavered on the threshold, tempted to apologise for inconveniencing him with her hobby. Then she reminded herself that she was mistress here, and he the intruder. She took a seat opposite him and gave him the firm schoolmistress smile she had been using on the other men.

'Have you come to send me to the country again? Because, as I told you, I would much prefer to remain in London.'

'I see that,' he said, then announced, 'I have come to apologise.' He looked down at his own empty hands and muttered, 'I should have brought a gift. Flowers, perhaps.'

'It is not that I do not like flowers,' she said. 'But I would much rather see them in the garden than plucked and brought here.'

'I see.' He frowned in confusion.

'But I enjoy that flowers in the house bring you pleasure,' she said with a smile, and for a moment she felt like her old shy self, ready to take up the watercolours and paintbrush to please him.

'If you enjoy the garden, perhaps you could come and visit it,' he suggested in a halting voice, as if he could not quite decide where to start.

'Perhaps I shall,' she agreed. She added, 'Some day when you are not at home.'

'Ahh.' For a moment he was lost for words, as she'd been so often in his presence. His posture straightened to be more contrite. His hands folded in his lap.

'But you were apologising,' she reminded him.

'I made a mistake,' he began.

She cut him off. 'I was aware of that from the first. You have made multiple mistakes, in my opinion. Which one are we talking about?'

He started, surprised. Then he beamed at her in approval, as if he was enjoying this new, bolder her. 'The one where I blamed you for the chaos that my life has been plunged into since we married,' he said. 'You are not at fault for the pandemonium. That was always there. You simply made me aware of it.'

She folded her arms and stared at him expectantly.

'My father's rules were nonsense,' he said, leaning forward as if about to reach for her. 'Ramsey was a thief. The necklace was always false and I didn't notice. And all women are not alike.'

'Really?' she said, feigning surprise.

'It is better that I know the truth,' he said. 'I do not like it, but it is better. It was wrong to blame you for the way you proved it to me.'

'Things cannot change until you know them for what they are,' she said encouragingly.

'I was wrong to blame you for lying to me and to complain that you didn't trust me, when I was hiding my feelings from you and from myself.'

'Your feelings?' she said cautiously, her new-found courage faltering.

'My love,' he said, with a soft coaxing smile. 'I did not even believe I had it to offer. But I was wrong about that as well. My life has changed for the better since I have come to know you, Maddie. You have all my love, and that is the proof.'

His love. She had waited so long to hear those words that she was unsure of how to answer.

'I am better off as well,' she said at last. 'And not just because you made me a duchess. It was not until you sent me away that I was forced to find the courage to be myself. And I like who I have become.'

'I like you as well,' he said, smiling hopefully.

'Do you?' she asked. 'Because I do not want to go back to the way I was when we were together, when I was afraid all the time. I will probably never be the woman you hoped for. I cannot be quiet and orderly and wear stuffy dresses and embroider your name in the corner of your handkerchiefs all evening, even if you read to me, which I quite enjoyed, by the way.' She ended the sentence in a gasp, as if it had used up the last of her breath to tell him the truth. 'Not the handkerchiefs but the reading, that is.'

'I am aware of that,' he said.

'I am tired of treading on eggshells and having to apologise for who I am. There is nothing wrong with me. I will make mistakes, I am sure, just as I did with the necklace. Sometimes I will still be frightened of you for no logical reason.' She shook her head in frustration. 'I have my father to thank for that. But I have told him that I do not wish to see him any more.'

'That was very brave of you,' Evan said with an encouraging smile. Then he paused, before he said, 'Is it bad to admit that you are more interesting now that I know that I have given up trying to control you? When I saw you at the ball last night…' He gave a confused shake of his head. 'It was as if I was seeing you for the first time.'

'I think you will find that life is more interesting when it is unpredictable,' she said, unable to hide her smile. 'More frightening, of course. But not terrifying. I think I am learning the difference.'

'Terror,' he said, frowning. 'Whether you come back to me or not, that part of your life is over. You will not be hurt by me or anyone else as long as I draw breath.'

'I know that,' she said. 'I think, in my heart, I knew it all along. Because I loved you from the moment we met. I saw you at the ball, and everything changed.'

'For me as well,' he said with a laugh.

'Because I fell on your head,' she said, rolling her eyes.

'And I arranged to marry you without asking,' he added, rising and taking a step towards her, arms outstretched.

'You had your honour to think of,' she reminded him, rising and stepping just out of his reach.

'It is not too late to change that,' he said, and dropped to a knee before her.

She laughed. 'I think it is. We are already married, you know.'

'But that does not mean I cannot give you the proposal you deserve,' he said, smiling and holding out his hands to her.

As always, she was unable to resist his smile. She stepped closer and took them in hers. Then she waited to see what would happen next.

'Miss Goddard,' he said, staring up into her eyes, 'you are the most captivating creature I have ever encountered.'

She laughed and tried to pull away. 'I find that hard to believe.'

'It is true,' he said, squeezing her hands. Then the words rushed out of him like rain from a breaking storm. 'I never thought that talk of mathematics could excite me. If we are speaking of terror, then you understand what I feel when faced with proofs and equations. But your lecture was the most exciting thing I have ever heard a woman say.'

'Exciting?' she said, raising a sceptical eyebrow.

He nodded. 'Very much so. I did not understand what you were saying, of course. It was like being wooed in a foreign tongue.'

'That was not the effect I was striving for,' she said.

'The other men there were equally enraptured. If I do not move quickly to secure a place in your affections, I shall be standing at the back of a very long line.'

'There is no one else,' she insisted.

'That is good to know. Because I do not think I can live without your muttering and scribbling and calculating. They are a part of you, and so they are part of me. I am lost without them, as I am lost without you. I love you, Maddie. Come back to me. Be my wife.'

She answered with a nod and pulled him to his feet, then stepped between his outstretched arms, fitting against his body as if she had always been a part of him.

'I couldn't leave, even when you tried to send me away. I cannot leave you now.'

'I am glad,' he replied, kissing her. Then he added, 'And Ramsey is gone from the house. You were right about him, of course. So I took the necessary action and am now without a bookkeeper.' He pulled back from her so that he could look into her eyes. 'Fortunately, I know just the person to take over the management of the accounts. And I will not even have to pay her, for she is already rich.'

'You would trust me with the estate?' she said, surprised.

'I would be a fool not to. I trust you with my life,

my love and my child. Why would I not allow you to do something that will give you more pleasure than it ever did me?'

She kissed him then, an open-mouthed kiss of utter happiness. 'That is the most interesting proposal I have ever received,' she said.

'The most interesting?' he said with a roguish grin and a shake of his head. Then he went to the door of the sitting room, closing it and turning the key in the lock. 'Wait until you hear what I propose we do next.'

* * * * *

COMING SOON!

We really hope you enjoyed reading this book. If you're looking for more romance be sure to head to the shops when new books are available on

Thursday 20th July

To see which titles are coming soon, please visit

millsandboon.co.uk/nextmonth

MILLS & BOON

MILLS & BOON®

Coming next month

A LAIRD WITHOUT A PAST
Jeanine Englert

Where are my clothes? Why am I naked?

What was going on?

A dog barked, and Royce lowered into a battle stance putting out his hands to defend his body.

'Easy, boy. Easy,' he commanded.

The dog barked again and nudged his wet nose to Royce's hand. Royce opened his palm, and the dog slathered his hand with its tongue and released a playful yip. Royce exhaled, his shoulders relaxing. He pet the dog's wiry hair and took a halting breath as his heart tried to regain a normal rhythm.

A latch clanked behind him followed by the slow, creaky opening of a door, and Royce whirled around to defend himself, blinking rapidly to clear his vision but still seeing nothing.

'Who are you?' he ordered, his voice stern and commanding as he felt about for a weapon, any weapon. His hand closed around what felt like a vase, and he held it high in the air. 'And how dare you keep me prisoner here. Release me!'

'Sailor's fortune' a woman cried. 'I think my soul left my body; you gave me such a fright. You are no prisoner,' a woman stated plainly. 'By all that's holy, cover yourself. And put down the vase. It was one of my mother's favourites.'

Light footfalls sounded away from him, but Royce stood poised to strike. He stared out into the darkness confused. Where was he and what was happening? And why was some woman speaking to him as if she knew him.

The door squeaked as it closed followed by the dropping of a latch.

'Then why am I here?' he demanded, still gripping the vase, unwilling to set it aside for clothes. Staying alive trumped any sense of propriety. She might not be alone.

'I cannot say. You were face down in the sand being stripped of your worldly possessions when I discovered you.' A pot clanged on what sounded to be a stove. 'Care to put on some trews? They are dry now.'

'Are you alone?' he asked, shifting from one foot to another staring out into the black abyss.

'Aye,' she chuckled.

He relaxed his hold on the vase, felt for the mattress, and sat down fighting off the light-headedness that made him feel weak in the knees.

'Could I trouble you to light a candle if you do not plan to kill me? I cannot see a blasted thing, and I would very much like to put on those trews you mentioned.'

Continue reading
A LAIRD WITHOUT A PAST
Jeanine Englert

Available next month
www.millsandboon.co.uk

MILLS & BOON

THE HEART OF ROMANCE

A ROMANCE FOR EVERY READER

MODERN
Prepare to be swept off your feet by sophisticated, sexy and seductive heroes, in some of the world's most glamourous and romantic locations, where power and passion collide.

HISTORICAL
Escape with historical heroes from time gone by. Whether your passion is for wicked Regency Rakes, muscled Vikings or rugged Highlanders, awaken the romance of the past.

MEDICAL
Set your pulse racing with dedicated, delectable doctors in the high-pressure world of medicine, where emotions run high and passion, comfort and love are the best medicine.

True Love
Celebrate true love with tender stories of heartfelt romance, from the rush of falling in love to the joy a new baby can bring, and a focus on the emotional heart of a relationship.

Desire
Indulge in secrets and scandal, intense drama and sizzling hot action with heroes who have it all: wealth, status, good looks…everything but the right woman.

HEROES
The excitement of a gripping thriller, with intense romance at its heart. Resourceful, true-to-life women and strong, fearless men face danger and desire - a killer combination!

To see which titles are coming soon, please visit

millsandboon.co.uk/nextmonth

JOIN US ON SOCIAL MEDIA!

Stay up to date with our latest releases, author news and gossip, special offers and discounts, and all the behind-the-scenes action from Mills & Boon...

 @millsandboon

 @millsandboonuk

 facebook.com/millsandboon

 @millsandboonuk

It might just be true love...